A Deaf Journey through Time:
In fifteen stories and two dreams

Henk Betten

A Deaf Journey through Time: In fifteen stories and two dreams

ISBN 978-90-806571-7-5

This book was first published in 1998 in Dutch by Henk Betten.

© Copyright 2018
Author: Henk Betten
Publisher: Maya de Wit – Sign Language Interpreting Consultancy
Copy editor: Judith Henstra
Cover: Vivian van Schagen
Back cover photograph: Fotoburo Ferdinand van der Duin

Table of contents

My enormous thanks go to my publisher Maya de Wit, the support received from the Vrienden van Effatha foundation, the edit by Book Helpline, and Vivian van Schagen, who made the cover illustrations. Much appreciation also to Gallaudet University Press, Ms. Ivey Wallace, for the permission of reprinting chapters 16 & 17 from 'Deaf Like Me'. Finally, I want to thank my wife Hetty and our children Marleen and Erik who give color to our lives.

Introduction

When I was a pupil at the Royal Institute for the Deaf H.D. Guyot in Groningen, the Netherlands (1942-1955), I was strongly influenced by an enthusiastic psychology student, H. Gosker. As an assistant leader of the boys' house, he used to share stories in sign language about the adventures of Tarzan. In likewise fashion, he told us about the news in the newspaper. As you can imagine, he was really popular among us boys, we were always pressing him to tell us more.

Mr. Gosker opened my mind to the power of storytelling and made me reconsider my future possibilities. At age sixteen, I was determined to become a journalist. Unfortunately, the deaf institutes in Europe at that time did little to encourage me (and other Deaf students) in such ambitions. I was trained and had to work as a furniture maker, which I did from 1955 until 1961. It was a frustrating period in my life and I was glad when I got the opportunity to work in an office at last.

In 1970 I decided to attend a course on writing short stories. I published several articles, including one about Henri Daniël Guyot (1753–1828), the Walloon clergyman from a Huguenot family who founded the famous institute for the Deaf in Groningen. Eventually, I went on to write several books from 1976 until today, all focusing on different aspects of Deafness and society.

I was born in 1938 and have been Deaf from birth. After my retirement in 1996 I volunteered as a librarian at the Royal Kentalis, now in Haren, in the Northern Netherlands. I am also a member of Deaf History International.

Having read extensively about deaf experiences throughout the centuries, I thought it would be nice to bundle some of these stories. Their common theme is Deafness but as you will see, the experience of being Deaf has many facets, from frustrating or even painful to positive and uplifting. You will find some stories from antiquity and from the Bible. Others were lifted from classic, canonical authors. You will also come across a few of my own reminiscences.

As we have stepped into the 21st century, where technology keeps opening up new opportunities, it is even possible to imagine a world where Deafness is not an obstacle at all. For now, such a future might still be a dream but it is crucial to have and cherish such dreams. They propel us toward a better tomorrow. That said, allow me to start you off with some bittersweet memories and tell you, in the first story, about my own experiences of speech therapy in the 1940s. Then we will take a wide detour across many ages and places to finally land, as promised, in two dreams. You are cordially invited to dream with me.

1.   Speech Therapy

"The deaf person must satisfy himself with the watching of minimal movements of the muscles (of a mouth); usually without any result; one is shown a very incomplete carcass of language; one is invited to dance with a skeleton." C.G. Postma and E.P. Fröhlich (1927), *"Lip-reading as foundation for the deaf education is totally unsuitable"* (page 50).

It was a rainy day in August 1942, when the family stood on the square before the big building: a man, a woman, and between them a small boy, three years of age, called Hendrik. They looked up at the imposing building, the Institute for the Deaf, with its commanding facade of red brick. Both parents sighed. They must leave their child at the boarding school. But Hendrik looked around untroubled and made sounds with his feet, which he himself couldn't hear. He had been deaf from birth, as had his elder sister Hiltje.

After about five minutes, the director of the Institute approached them. He was a man with a face that reflected strictness. He looked appraisingly at Hendrik, and then he said, "Well, Well, Well."

"Yes," replied Mr. Meesters, Hendrik's father.

"Where is Hiltje, your daughter?"

"She is ill, sir. Flu," said the father, Mr. Meesters.

"That's all right. When will she come back?"

"Next week, I hope, sir."

The director nodded and invited the family to inspect the building, which was only for little boys. They walked through a hallway, the walls clad with shiny tiles, and then on to the courtyard. In the building, Mr. and Mrs. Meesters spoke with Miss Tiel, the group leader who looked friendly with her silver-gray hair.

"What's his name?" she asked, pointing at Hendrik.

The boy looked up at her, impressed by her appearance when she made the gesture.

The usual formalities were exchanged, and the visitors and the director walked across the same courtyard through the hallway to a classroom. They looked inside the room, which was empty. The new school year was to start the next day.

It was time for Mr. and Mrs. Meesters to leave. Miss Tiel tried to interest Hendrik in playing with the toys in the boys' house. He played with a few boys, but he felt unhappy and turned away. Gradually, however, his fear and distrust disappeared. Miss Tiel noticed it and nodded at the parents that this was a good time to leave.

That was easier said than done. Mrs. Meesters hesitated but her husband pulled her arm softly. "Come."

They left the room, where the boys played silently.

After a while, Hendrik looked up from the toys and searched the room. His parents had left! He panicked. Quickly, Miss Tiel approached the little boy to comfort him but that only made things worse. He ran to the door, but he wasn't tall enough to reach the handle. That made him very angry, and he stamped his feet furiously on the wooden floor.

The other boys looked at his tears with amazement. Some boys realized that they too had been separated from their parents and they began crying. The group leader shook her head because of all the sadness, and she thought, "Where have I ever seen such a vale of tears?"

The next day, together with other boys and girls of his age, and the teacher in a classroom, Hendrik had a completely new experience. A figure in a brown jacket came through the door. His face was tanned from the sun. The man beckoned to Hendrik with his index finger and Hendrik remembered the meaning of this gesture. He had learned this sign from Hiltje. So, he got out of his seat and walked over to the man without hesitation.

"Amazing!" said the man to his colleague, who sat in front of the pupils. "He's only been here a day and yet he understands."

"He seems promising. You're right. I'll keep an eye on him," the teacher replied.

Then the man in the brown jacket softly pushed Hendrik into the hallway and closed the classroom door. The man turned out to be the speech therapist.

"Well, Hendrik, I am sure we will become good friends, but only if you can help me," the speech therapist said. But Hendrik only saw his lips move a little. They entered a small room. A big mirror was placed against the wall. The boy saw himself and smiled. He liked looking at himself and expected more fun. The teacher got out a wooden plank with a groove along its length. Hendrik had to blow a little ball from one end to the other. He loved it and wanted to keep playing the game.

This game was to develop his breathing to allow him to learn to speak. Since his birth, Hendrik had used very little or no voice, so his voice needed to be activated. Within a few weeks, Hendrik had learned how to make several sounds. It had not been easy. Hendrik put his hand on the teacher's throat to feel the movements, which for him, had been quite frightening.

One day the teacher decided it was time for Hendrik to utter his first word: "Mammy." His parents came in the morning to visit him and Hiltje. It had been a while, and Hendrik burst into tears at the first sight of his parents, because he had missed them so much.

The teacher put a photograph of Hendrik's mother on the ledge in front of the mirror. Again, Hendrik started weeping. The teacher then put the boy on his knee. That helped.

"Mammy, mammy," the teacher started, but his pupil just stared at him blankly. Patiently the man took the little hand and placed it on his throat. Hendrik again felt aversion, particularly because of the huge size of the man's Adam's apple.

"Mammy…"

Hendrik wanted to come down from the teacher's knee. It was too much for him.

The teacher brought the boy to the classroom of another teacher.

In the following weeks, Hendrik made little progress. His teacher was desperate. As a renowned speech therapist, he had a reputation to uphold in several European countries. At home, with his wife, formerly a teacher in mainstream education, he spoke about his problems with Hendrik.

"He certainly has it in him to learn to speak, but so far he does not want to cooperate."

His wife looked at him over her knitting and thought for a while. Her husband looked intently at her face, which was so full of concentration. She said, "Ah, poor Hendrik. You have not tormented him too much?"

"What?! I wouldn't do such a thing!"

She fell into a muse and the speech therapist looked expectantly at her face.

"I have a suggestion, but I do not know if you will like it when I say it."

"Machteld, please say what you think."

"I get the impression that it takes the pupils a lot of effort to learn to talk. They are not allowed to use sign language. Can they not learn it while making gestures to each other?"

"Sure, they do that. You should see it yourself: so many hand movements and a lot of enthusiasm. I picked up the sign language for myself, even though the director strictly forbade it."

10

"So, so, you see," his wife said enigmatically.

"Say, woman, what do you mean by that? What are you saying?" The voice of her husband sounded unusually sharp. "Are we not doing our best?" the tormented teacher continued.

"Yes, that's for sure. And you are famous after all, but as far as Hendrik is concerned, I have the feeling that, if and when he does learn to speak, he might ask, 'Why did you make us go through all this trouble? Such a waste of time and energy; why so much effort for our language development?'"

She bravely continued, "I think Hendrik is homesick and feels a lot of stress. And now that I think about it, why is it so terribly important to teach deaf children to speak? It's like for them at the way as Via Dolorosa, and perhaps yours too."

The comfortable room was filled with icy silence.

"You think that you know how to educate the deaf? No!"

He grabbed his pipe and smoked. His wife saw his hands tremble in frustration.

One day, Hendrik returned from the visiting room where his parents had spent half an hour with him and Hiltje. He was homesick and sat on a seat with some other boys, staring into space. Suddenly he felt the ticking of a stick on the wooden floor. This continual ticking sound became louder and it annoyed Hendrik. His eyes searched the room to see who or what was causing it. A fat boy in the corner was holding a stick and he pounded it on the wooden floor. Hendrik ran toward him and took the stick from him. A few moments later they were fighting. Miss Tiel, attracted by the noise, walked up to them. Her hand hit the boys several times.

Then, to Miss Tiel's surprise, Hendrik began to cry, louder and louder. It made him retch, so she took him to the toilet. The content of his stomach and all the homesickness of the past months disappeared into the bowl. A bit later, he seemed fine again. It was decided that he would be allowed to see Hiltje every other day in the courtyard. He badly needed contact with his family. The next day, the teacher saw Hendrik in the hallway.

It's now or never, he thought.

The persistent teacher gently steered Hendrik to a chair and the lesson began. On the blackboard were pictures of Mr. and Mrs. Meesters and Hendrik's brothers and sisters. The manicured index finger of the teacher pointed to the word on the picture, while his mouth slowly articulated the words.

"Daddy, daddy, mammy, mammy, mammy."

For the first time, Hendrik really looked at what the teacher was doing.

The following words came out his mouth! "Muuuuuuuummm…" And again: "Muuuuuuuummm."

The teacher jumped up joyfully and Hendrik laughed with a big smile on his face. The teacher grabbed him and lifted him up. In the mirror, Hendrik saw himself sitting on the shoulders of the teacher. He screamed with joy. Never had he had so much fun as on this day.

When Mr. and Mrs. Meesters arrived on the last day in November, they heard their son clearly speak the words, "Mammy, daddy" in his own particular way.

Source:
My father and my imagination of what may have happened.

2.   The Fable of the Fox and the Duck

In the forest, the fox is looking for prey. Suddenly, he catches sight of a solitary duck. The duck is unsuspectingly basking in the sunlight at the edge of the lake.

Then the fox hears a couple of ducks warn the duck on the ground with loud quacking. It amazes the fox that the duck is not in the least alarmed by it. He hesitates.

On a branch a raven, that has been watching, suddenly asks, "Reynard, why don't you catch that duck?"

"Me? Well, I was going to, but the duck doesn't seem to be afraid of me. Isn't that strange?"

The raven laughs out loud. "That's not strange. That duck is deaf!"

Still, the fox does not make any attempt to jump at the duck. It amazes the raven, who then asks again, "Why don't you devour her? Doesn't she look nice and fat?"

"Well," the fox answers, "what if deafness is contagious?"

3. The Curse

It was late afternoon, somewhere near the Mount Sinai, when suddenly clouds filled the sky. It seemed as if night had come, it was so dark. Suddenly it stormed. And then a bolt of lightning appeared, casting the surroundings in a miraculous light.

In front of the entrance to her tent sat a woman, a widow, who was terribly frightened by the change in the weather. She looked at her son.

"Where would Asram be, you think?" she exclaimed. "I hope he's not hiding under the large acacia shrub."

Hear, the storm roared. The old woman hastily crept into the tent because she knew all too well that sand penetrates everything and she wanted to protect her eyes. Now and then, she peered outside through a narrow crack.

Asram was twenty years old and unable to speak because he had been deaf probably from birth. Some years ago, in Egypt, his father had died lonely in the middle of his fellow sufferers who all had leprosy. The woman called her other son for help.

Despite the noise of the storm, he heard her and he walked immediately through the door of the tent and asked, "What is it, Mother?"

"Where is Asram?"

"I don't know. Shall I go and look for him?"

"Yes, my son, please. You know that this severe weather outside is much too dangerous for Asram. In any case, he is not allowed to hide under the large acacia shrub."

"Oh, Mother. Asram isn't stupid. But, well, I will look for him and if I see him, I will send him to you."

"Okay, my son."

With a smile, she watched him go.

Asram returned to the tent before it was completely dark outside. His mother had the feeling that he was not very impressed by the storm: his face didn't show it. Just like every other day, he looked so unaffected and expressionless.

Only when he laughed, it was different. Then he looked very much like his only sister, Ephrata.

Last week something terrible had happened. On the hottest day of the season, Ephrata came to her mother, crying.

"What is it, my daughter. Why do you cry?" her mother asked.

Her sobs were her only answer. The widow waited patiently for her child to calm down.

"It's really terrible," Ephrata said.

"Take it easy. What happened? Tell me!"

"Well, I stood by Uncle Maehal's fireplace, and Jasai suddenly became furious at our Asram. I heard Jasai cursing because of Asram's deafness!"

"Our cousin Jasai cursed our Asram?"

"Yes, I heard it myself. Terrible. But Asram cannot hear and doesn't even realize that his cousin cursed him."

Ephrata started sobbing again. The widow stared at her in silence and then put her hands to her face.

Some women came to the door to find out why and for whom they were weeping.
Old Miriam had also heard the appalling news. She immediately ran, quite fast given her age, to Moses' tent.

Through the entrance of the tent she saw her brother having an afternoon nap. Her mood changed to tenderness.

"Oh well," Miriam thought. "Yesterday Moses had been on a trip far away and now he was obviously still tired. I better wait a little longer."

She dawdled. But what about Asram? He had to be helped! Of course, her cousin's family felt deeply grieved by the Jasai's curse.

Why had he done that? It would be best if her brother, as the leader of the Israelites, attended to such matters himself.

She softly called Moses. First it seemed that the brother to whom she had felt a bond since the time they were children, would continue to sleep. But then suddenly, Moses stood there in front of her in his full length.

"Miriam!" his clear voice sounded.

They greeted each other with a smile and Miriam told him that she had something to say.

"Then join us," Moses said. "It's almost dinner time."

He called the slave of his wife, Zipporah, and told her that Miriam would eat with them. Moments later they ate and drank goat's meat and sheep's milk together with Zipporah. Miriam began her story about Jasai's curse. Moses saw outrage in the eyes of his sister.

He understood her agitation and replied, "Well, tomorrow morning I will go to Maehal and ask him why Jasai did that."

"Moses, I am sorry, but our cousin is so upset. Maybe it would be better for her if you would go to her brother now."

She was usually able to persuade him to do what she wanted. His mother had told him that Miriam had taken very good care of him when he was found as a baby in a wicker basket lying between the reeds in the river Nile. In addition, Miriam was much loved by the people.

"Well, Miriam, you get what you want," Moses said with a smile. He took his stick off the ground, and with his feet in sandals went on his way to Maehal. "Why did Jasai do that?" Moses wondered. He usually didn't cause any trouble. Swearing to Asram because of his deafness was outrageous, but Moses had himself wondered whether it would be wise to punish Jasai in public. All of a sudden, Moses remembered a blind man.

A few years ago, some bad boys put thick branches before the feet of this man. He stumbled over them while the bystanders laughed loudly.

Some distance from the tents in the camp, Moses paused for a moment and he prayed to God for wisdom.

Maehal was surprised when Moses, his cousin, stood before the entrance of his tent in person. "Shalom, cousin Maehal," said the visitor with a serious face. Maehal invited him to sit down.

Moses asked him quickly, "Maehal, do you know what happened this afternoon?"

"No... Yes. I heard only the weeping of women."

The two men in their stripy clothes remained silent for a while.

Moses stared at the tent that was made from goat's hairs and asked, "Will you ask Jasai to come here and talk to us?"

A little later, Jasai said with an innocent face, "Me? I cursed him because of his deafness?"

Moses and Maehal looked at Jasai.

"Jasai, will you ask Ephrata, your cousin, to come here as a witness?"

That was more than enough to make Jasai confess that he had done it. He had a soft spot for Ephrata. He hoped to have her as his wife in the future. But now he was ashamed of what he'd done.

Moses asked, "What happened?"

The young man sighed deeply and said after some hesitation: "The last few days, Asram has been acting strangely. I noticed that this afternoon he threw some branches of acacia wood on our fireplace although that is banned, isn't it?"

"Yes," said his mother. "I had asked Asram to pick up some branches for the fire. He always did this gladly. And of course, I was as surprised as Jasai when I found this wood in the fireplace."

Moses stared ahead for a while. It was now all clear. This acacia wood was intended only for the altar of the Ark of the Lord. Together with his brother, Moses had given the order. But Asram, as a deaf man, could not know. Lots of things such as news and new laws for the people of Israel passed him by. He could only understand gestures about things such as eating, sleeping, etc.

"Jasai, Jasai, you must never curse. Will you promise me?"

The young man bowed deeply and nodded while blushing.

"Jasai, go straight to your aunt and her family and ask them for forgiveness!"

The young man quickly stood up and he ran to the tent of Asram's family to do what Moses had ordered.

Source:
"You shall not curse the deaf or put a stumbling block before the blind, but you shall fear your God: I am the LORD." Leviticus 19:14 (English Standard Version)

4.   Mime and Sand Writing

In the year 535 BC, Euricles arrived in Eleusis in the province of Attica during one of his wanderings. In the market square, this sparingly dressed young man looked around him, and his eye fell on a little bird with a bouncy tail, that stood on the head of a gray statue.

The young man enjoyed watching until the bird flew away. Only then did he have good look at the stone statue. The head was so expressive! Curiously, he ran forward to get a better look. His gaze slid down and he carefully studied the position of the two strong arms of the torso. One was quite straight while the other curved down strongly. Then he took a few steps back again. The huge feet rested on a plinth of marble. Euricles thought, *this is great!*

Suddenly he took exactly the same pose as that of the statue. He remained standing there for a while. He found it rather amazing that he did so, and so he did it one more time.

Forgotten was the quiet grief that he carried inside. When he had been fifteen years old, he had fallen off a horse, and hit his head on a tree trunk, very hard. Out of nowhere, he became deaf. In all other respects, he recovered quickly, but his hearing was lost for good. Euricles made the unpleasant discovery that the people, including his family, hardly had the patience or made any effort to talk to him, although he could use his voice. The people did not know how to react. In fact, what he said fell on deaf ears! The people began to bypass him and he felt more and more isolated and left to his own devices. After a while, he got used to living on his own but it still hurt inside.

The game with the statue stayed in his thoughts. When on his trip he arrived at the capital of Attica, he quickly searched the dozens of statues of the gallery, large and small, that the city is so famous for. One after the other, he tried to imitate statues' facial expressions and poses. Sometimes it was easy, sometimes more difficult, but he felt good. A huge joy welled up in Euricles. He wanted to dance!

But after a few steps his feeling of joy left him. Dance? Music? Never more! He was angered and deeply disappointed and it resonated in his head: *Why I am deaf?*

Suddenly Euricles saw that he was no longer alone in the gallery.

A group of people stood there talking. Who they were, he did not know but it seemed as if they were quarrelling. They moved their arms so violently! He approached shyly but curious, but suddenly his gaze was drawn to a statue. It was next to the gallery on the square. Mighty arms reached up. Immediately he imitated this pose too. It worked well and he stayed in this pose for a long time.

Unintentionally he drew the attention of the people. When he turned around to continue his walk, he saw an obese man in the group who had taken the same frozen pose. Funny! Euricles began to laugh. The stranger laughed broadly with Euricles, still holding his pose.

Then suddenly that fat man looked so angry that the deaf young man immediately showed a startled face. That was the intention of Thespis, the stranger. He wanted to show an expression on his face that would invoke a response, a change of facial expression. The spectators were now standing around Euricles and Thespis; they looked captivated by this new game, that we now call pantomime.

Thespis was the first to stop and he wanted to talk to Euricles. But Euricles shook his head and put his index fingers in his ears while his face looked sad.

Thespis at first looked surprised but then he realized that Euricles was deaf. He beckoned Euricles to join him and in a quiet spot the older man wrote something in the sand with his index finger. Euricles watched and recognized the words, and a cry of joy came from his mouth. This was the solution to his communication problem!

Euricles replied with his own voice and Thespis could understand him well. Thespis wrote in the sand that he enjoyed what they had just discovered together—that one can tell stories with body and face and can express feelings without any human sound.

Thespis decided to further explore this new form of human expression with Euricles. Euricles stayed with his older friend for a long time; they became good friends. The sand remained willing and they became skilled at their pantomime performances. This way, they traveled all over Greece. Euricles felt like a complete human being again.

5. How Gedaliah Found His Brother Back

It was a day to remember, at that desolate place. Many people witnessed a spectacular event, that Gedaliah, as a prosperous caravan merchant, was very pleased with. That is why he ordered his slaves to prepare a feast and to invite his entire family and all his friends.

When all the guests were present for the meal, consisting of a fattened calf, legs of lamb, and fruits, Gedaliah saw to his horror that his brother was missing.

In a whisper, he asked his slave where Manasseh was. The slave said that he had seen him going toward the lake. Gedaliah nodded and sighed a deep sigh of shame. A party without his brother as the center point was not what he had in mind. Annoyed, he ran to his place at the table and he told the guests that it may be some time before Manasseh arrived. He felt the look of his father on him and wondered how he should entertain guests for so long.

Luckily, his neighbor came to his aid by asking about the special event that Manasseh had been involved in. So, all eyes were on Gedaliah, full of anticipation, and he suddenly realized that this was an opportunity to tell the unique story.

While talking he forgot his sense of shame about the absence of his brother. In the torch-lit room of his large house in Hippus, a town in Decapolis, everyone listened attentively to his story:

In the days of Emperor Tiberius, a farmer lived in peace with his faithful wife. He worked in a fertile area that used to be called Basan. They prospered. Their only desire, however, was to have a child. For ten years they had hoped for the fulfillment of that desire. The Jewish woman prayed to her God every day. And this aroused the mockery of her unbelieving husband time and again. But one day the woman felt that the birth of a child seemed to be imminent.

Every day she secretly felt with her hand on her belly to check that it was not a dream. No, she now knew with great certainty that she was expecting a child, but she still did not dare to talk to her husband about it. But he did notice her shining eyes, and in silence he wondered what the reason could be. It seemed to take a long time before the child was finally born, which turned out to be a boy. The farmer saw this event with surprise and, together with his wife, praised the goodness of the God of Israel. They gave their son the name Gedaliah, which means, 'Yahweh has shown himself great'.

Gedaliah looked at the people present, smiling broadly as he listened to tell whether his brother was arriving yet. He wasn't and so Gedaliah went on with his story:

While Gedaliah was growing up, his mother waited a long time to have another child. How pleased she was when that happy event announced itself. As a descendant of the patriarch Jakob, she wanted her second child to be called Manasseh. Unfortunately, the woman died a few days after the birth of her son. Gedaliah, then eight years old, was so confused that he fled.

For several days he wandered through the area and climbed hill after hill. He felt so lost, especially because his father did not pay any attention to him during those sad days.

Yet one day the boy returned to his father who took him in his arms in silence. To his surprise, Gedaliah saw a tear glisten in the sunlight in the black-gray beard of his father.

Some years went by and slowly Gedaliah discovered that his brother looked a lot like his mother. That made him love him a lot more and he gave all his attention to little Manasseh, who in turn enjoyed the presence of his big brother.

Gedaliah's father made him work hard. He herded a flock of sheep and goats in the fields. Manasseh occasionally came along. Gedaliah also had to help on the farm, with the cattle, sheep and the donkeys.

To the great amazement of Gedaliah's father, the herd gradually expanded. He thought, *maybe the God of Israel does exist? Maybe my wife was right. I should have listened to her better instead of mocking her God.*

One day, a caravan merchant came to talk to the farmer about the sale of part of his flock of sheep. Not long afterwards, Gedaliah, now an adult, was commissioned by his father to accompany a flock of sheep with his fellow countrymen all the way to Jericho in the land of Palestine. This was to help the caravan merchant. When Gedaliah heard of his assignment, he jumped for joy. He had been attracted to distant travels since his boyhood. The wait was now on the arrival of the large caravan from Damascus.

Every day Gedaliah stood on the lookout on one of the highest hills in the ten cities region called Decapolis. One hot morning, the moment finally arrived. Excited, he ran to his father to tell him that the caravan was in sight.

"How far, my son?" his father asked without looking up from his work.

"Um, I think the caravan can be here in the afternoon."

With difficulty the farmer got up from his stooped position and he threw his razor to the side, leaving a half-shaved sheep behind. Appraisingly, his eyes passed over the sheep, while he walked quietly. Then he drove the best sheep out of the herd and Gedaliah was told to keep those sheep separate for the time being."

In the afternoon, the Syrian merchant came to see the sheep. Gedaliah joined the men. Hear, the money sounded. Would his father get a lot of money?

At last the moment came to say goodbye. It was not easy for Gedaliah to leave Manasseh behind. It also felt as if he was now saying goodbye to his deceased mother, who was buried here after all. He quickly turned around and walked with the sheep toward the caravan.

That is how Manasseh saw his big brother leave. Slowly, the procession of known and unknown people became smaller and smaller until only a dust cloud could be seen.

About three years later, Gedaliah, almost unrecognizable with his full beard, returned to his father and brother. He first spotted Manasseh. Of course, he called him by his name, but to his surprise, Manasseh did not turn around. That was weird. Once again, he called as hard as possible, 'Manasseh!'

Nothing worked. *Strange*, he thought, troubled. *Could Manasseh still be angry because I left?*

When Gedaliah came up to his brother, he gave him a fraternal pat on the shoulder. But the only result was a mortally frightened look in Manasseh's eyes.

Manasseh then embraced his brother. He held him so long during the embrace that Gedaliah had the feeling that Manasseh had really missed him. But what a strange voice Manasseh had. It seemed as if it was difficult for him to speak.

Their father came from behind the tent and at first didn't recognize his eldest son. Gedaliah, however, rushed toward him and embraced him tenderly. After they both inquired about each other's health and well-being in the shady tent, the farmer stared blankly ahead of him.

Gedaliah waited and suddenly his father said, "Tell me, my son, do you already know about Manasseh?"

Gedaliah shook his head and frowned. What could his father mean?

"Manasseh has not been able to hear since about a year and a half ago."

"What?" was the only thing Gedaliah could utter. He could not quite imagine what it was like to not be able to hear. The farmer continued, "It's a disaster; I cannot talk to Manasseh anymore. Gedaliah, did you hear what I said? He does not belong anymore."

The farmer screamed so hard that Gedaliah drew back in alarm.

"Call Manasseh, call him, my son, by his name."

Gedaliah looked at his father in surprise but complied with his request and called his brother. Manasseh sat with his back to them and did not respond. As if hit by lightning, Gedaliah did not say anything for a long time.

"How awful this is; first mother dead and now this," Gedaliah said.

The farmer looked sadly at his eldest son and said, "I am still wondering how something like this could just happen. Maybe it's a punishment from the God of Israel, because I used to mock your mother for her faith."

Those present all looked at Gedaliah's father. They watched as his beard trembled from emotion and they heard him sigh deeply. Gedaliah resumed his story with a veiled smile:

The hated Romans were still there, and Emperor Tiberius ruled with a heavy hand. People in Hippos often talked about it. They grumbled about the high taxes and this happened everywhere. Gedaliah had some experience of this.

He too hated the tax collectors, who often added an extra levy on top of the taxes they had to collect and put it into their own pockets.

As a caravan merchant, Gedaliah often went along the borders of Galilee, Samaria, Judea, and Idumea. According to him, the Jewish tax collectors, with Zacheus as their boss in Jericho, went too far. It was pure extortion.

When he returned to Hippos again after a few years on a caravan trip, he heard startling news. His father told him in great color and detail how an unknown physician from Palestine liberated a possessed Gadara from the clutches of an evil spirit.

After his father finished speaking, Gedaliah asked cynically, "Have you seen it yourself?"

The whole story was rather unbelievable for Gedaliah.

"No, it's not like that, my son. It was told by your uncle from Abila and later by the man who is healed. He has been here and now in his right mind. I used to hear him scream and rant and I saw him roam the Gadara cemetery."

Gedaliah still did not believe it, and when his father realized this, he exclaimed, "To Isis, have I ever lied to you?"

"No, no, my father," Gedaliah hastened to say. However, it annoyed him that his father still used this religious expression. Suddenly things began to dawn on Gedaliah and, falteringly, he asked, "That unknown physician, would he be able to … heal our Manasseh?"

His father bowed his head and nodded briefly. Gedaliah continued to dwell on the thought and imagined how wonderful it would be if the unknown man could give Manasseh back his hearing.

"Well, it's probably not possible anyway," said his father. "Have you heard about that Persian miracle doctor?"

Gedaliah shook his head and so his father told the story about how that doctor had tried to bring a dead person to life and how that failed.

"And then?" Gedaliah insisted. "My son, the people who witnessed that failure, did not settle for it and stoned the unfortunate Persian."

While Gedaliah thought about that outrageous cruelty, an Ethiopian house slave approached with soft footsteps. He put tin cups on the table and removed himself in the same silent way. The older man took a cup and drank the wine in a few sips.

"What now?" he grumbled as he saw the slave again. However, the man bowed deeply and announced a visitor.

"Well, let him come in."

Gedaliah saw his father's brother-in-law appear at the entrance and heard him say, "Shalom." His father's face showed some emotion that did not escape Gedaliah's attention.

Gedaliah also greeted the visitor: "Shalom, Uncle Gershom."

After some introductory words, the visitor, dressed in Palestinian costume, began to talk about the miraculous physician who lived in his country.

"That man, as true as I am here, has a very peculiar power, and I do not talk about money or politics, oh no."

With his finger, the guest meaningfully tapped his temple a few times.

"It is whispered that the rabbis are feeling inferior in the presence of this man, Jesus of Nazareth. He could be a prophet. What am I saying, prophet? Lo and behold, that could be it. He could be the long-awaited Messiah himself."

The eyes of Gershom shone strangely.

"Yes, well, those rabbis in their long coats …" Gedaliah said mockingly.

His laughter soon faded, however, when his father snapped at him, "Shut up. Did Uncle Gershom tell you to speak up?"

Gedaliah made a repentant face, but in the meantime thought how hopelessly old-fashioned his father actually was. He missed the extended views of a well-traveled man, that was clear.

The slave put a bowl of Persian figs on the table, and Gedaliah took a few. As he slowly chewed the fruit, he pondered, would it be possible for that prophet to heal Manasseh's deafness?

He sighed deeply and let his brown eyes wander. He saw Manasseh leaning against the wall. He radiated boredom. He just stood there and stared into the distance.

People avoided him. It seemed like he was a leper … Gedaliah missed his mother a lot. She would have known what to do. Actually, it was unbearable, this silence around Manasseh.

And the worst was the feeling of alienation that Gedaliah felt toward his brother. For him and perhaps for his father, Manasseh was only a living corpse.

He could not forget the tormented expression on Manasseh's face when Gedaliah had returned home from his last trip. And now there was this story about the cure of a possessed man.

Gedaliah decided to keep his eyes and ears open when he was traveling again. He needed to find out where this Jesus of Nazareth was staying. And then he, Gedaliah, would take his brother to him.

Suddenly his train of thought was interrupted by the approach of Selassie, his slave, who said, "My lord, there is someone outside who wants to speak to you."

"Who is it?"

"My lord, he says he is your friend. He is dressed in white and …"

"Ah, that must be Salem. Let him come in at once."

A tall man who was as old as Gedaliah approached and embraced his friend.

While they were talking to each other, Salem suddenly said, "Have you heard about that Jewish healer?"

"Yes, yes, my uncle just mentioned him too."

"He is now in our neighborhood," Salem exclaimed enthusiastically.

"No, really!" Gedaliah exclaimed in surprise. "Where is he exactly?"

"There, be," Salem pointed with his hand in the western direction.

"Near that hill."

Gedaliah was looking quietly at his friend; his brain worked at full speed. Suddenly he shouted loudly for his father, who immediately appeared at the stairs leading to the flat roof.

"What is it, my son?" Only then did he see Salem, who stood up from where he lay. He immediately forgot his question and the two men took some time to greet each other. Gedaliah could hardly wait until the usual ritual of the greeting was finished.

"My father, Jesus is close by."

The old man barely reacted, giving Gedaliah the impression that the words did not get through to his father.

"My father, you know who I mean. He is …"

The old man's face now showed interested and he asked, "Near here, you say? And do you want to go there?"

Gedaliah nodded and wondered why his father did not want to join straight away.

"Would it be possible for him to make Manasseh hear again? What do you think, Salem?" asked the father.

"I certainly believe that, my lord. I have been told that he gave the possessed man his mind back. It was amazing."

"Yes, yes, we know about that," the old man replied.

Gedaliah felt his heart pounding with joy. This morning he had had such a strange, light feeling, as if something very special was about to happen. Would this be it?

"My father, are not you coming?"

"Well, do you really think I'd stay here at home? Your mother would not forgive me if she was alive. So, let's go now. Wait, I'll ask Gershom to come along."

Gedaliah laughed freely. He already felt some of the silent desperation about his brother's deafness subside. Gedaliah looked confidently to the future and imagined what it would be like to be able to talk to Manasseh again.

It was annoying, however, that he could not explain to him now why they were all suddenly. Anyway, Gedaliah thought, that would only be short-lived. Manasseh would soon be able to understand everything again.

After a while, the whole family walked out into the bright sunlight. Salem also came along, because he was very curious to see whether Manasseh would soon be able to live a normal life again.

They joined the group of the people which moved slowly.

"Hey, Salem, did you see that Jewish prophet heal the sick with your own eyes?" Gedaliah asked, as they approached the rugged land after hours of walking.

"No, I heard about it from others who have experienced it up close."

"But how did that work?"

"Eh, they said he put his hands on those of the sick, like you often see miracle doctors do."

"And nothing else?" Gedaliah asked, amazed.

Salem shook his head. *Strange*, Gedaliah thought. *What will it be like when we speak to Jesus of Nazareth?* Gedaliah was very reluctant to speak to Jesus, but he knew Manasseh had to be cured one way or another. Just before night fell, the group arrived in the hills.

"Salem, look, what a mass of people," Gedaliah exclaimed.

Salem laughed with all his white teeth exposed. "Listen," he called out a moment later.

Loud and powerful was the voice of Jesus when he spoke in Aramaic:

"Come all to me who are weary and burdened; I will give you rest."

Gedaliah stood in the loose sand as if paralyzed. Then it felt as if something slipped away from him and peace descending into his mind. A moment later he noticed that people were starting to search for a suitable place to sleep.

That was a disappointment. Now it was too late. Jesus would leave tomorrow morning. Or even tonight?

But soon it became clear to him that Jesus would stay, and Gedaliah went looking for a place to sleep.

His father and his uncle and also Manasseh immediately prepared to go to sleep on their rolled-out mats. But Gedaliah and his friend wanted to walk. They approached a group of men sitting separately from the people on the slope of the hill and they found the courage to speak to one of the men.

The person addressed, a man with bright but friendly eyes, told them that Jesus was nearby and that he was tired and wanted to rest.

Gedaliah and Salem returned to the family reassured and also laid themselves to sleep. The night was in darkness. Here and there a fire flared up to keep the wild animals at a distance.

As soon as the sunlight touched Gedaliah's face, he woke up and again felt that happy feeling inside. Jesus of Nazareth was nearby. Gedaliah stood up, wrapped his cloak around him and woke his family. Together they walked past the people who were still asleep to the where the group of men were lying. Gedaliah bowed and introduced himself and his family.

"Simon bar Jonah," the man called himself. "Come and sit with us."

"Are you perhaps the son of Jonah of Bethsaida?" Gedaliah asked.

Simon nodded in the affirmative and Gershom joined in the conversation because he knew Simon's father well. Thus, the ice between the disciple of Jesus and the family was quickly broken. Simon heard Gedaliah's story about Manasseh with great interest and told him that Jesus would surely arrive soon. He was in prayer somewhere else at the moment.

The family kept on walking and started a conversation here and there. Suddenly, Gedaliah saw the man in white, standing alone on the hillside. That had to be Jesus. Now or never, Gedaliah thought, and he brought his family together. Jesus spoke, but Gedaliah did not allow himself the time to listen to him.

With his group he made his way to the front row and after some hesitation he headed straight for Jesus. That produced some mumbling along the lines of, "Let the prophet talk," and "What do those cursed dogs imagine?" and "Do they just think they can just walk to the front?"

Gedaliah heard it and became uncertain at once, but his eyes met a friendly, inviting
face. The family, except Manasseh, bowed deeply before the preacher and Gedaliah asked nervously, "My lord, my brother cannot hear and finds it hard to speak. Could you cure him of his deafness?"

Jesus looked at Manasseh, who looked around with little interest, but Jesus did not say anything. Gedaliah wondered about that and asked again, begging that he would put his hands-on Manasseh.

Jesus, however, walked to Manasseh without speaking and led him to a quiet spot next to an acacia bush. But Manasseh suddenly stood stock-still and looked back at his family. Gedaliah nodded reassuringly.

Gedaliah did not understand why the healer and his brother removed themselves from the crowd, but he did see how Jesus stuck his fingers in Manasseh's ears. What could that mean? To his surprise, he saw his brother nodding in understanding. Yes, that was it! Jesus wanted to make it clear to him by making a few gestures that he knew he was deaf. Ah, how stupid we were, Gedaliah thought. We could also have made gestures, but we never did.

The family saw even more: Jesus spat in his palm and touched Manasseh's tongue with his saliva. Gedaliah did not understand it. Salem then whispered in his friend's ear that he had seen it with other miracle doctors.

Then Jesus looked up at the sky and he sighed deeply. Gedaliah did not shake his head in understanding. Suddenly Gedaliah remembered his mother's stories about the God of Israel who lives in heaven and created heaven and earth. That prophet certainly had something to do with that God.

Then Gedaliah heard Jesus say the word "Ephphatha!" loud and clear.

What could this mean? Gedaliah made an effort to hear what was said at a great distance. He really thought he was hearing Manasseh's voice. Then he saw his brother approaching. His face looked so bright and much younger, Gedaliah thought in amazement. It seemed as if his brother had risen from the grave.

Gedaliah wanted to stretch out his arms to embrace Manasseh but stopped in time. He gave that honor to his father, who was standing next to him and was actually crying. Finally, it was his turn to embrace his brother.

Manasseh said with a clear sounding voice, "My father and my brother Gedaliah, how glad I am." Gedaliah nodded speechlessly and Manasseh continued, "I can now hear well again. It's wonderful."

The tears fell down Gedaliah's cheeks and a great joy sounded in his heart. He, too, felt overwhelmed that something like this could happen.

Gedaliah looked at the party people and was silent. Manasseh arrived at that moment. A cheer rose that reached the ears of the cheerfully smiling Manasseh.

Gedaliah called his name and said, "You can see that we celebrate, especially for you."

Manasseh looked rather shy and stayed in between his father and brother.

"Where have you been?" Gedaliah asked curiously.

"I was again with Jesus of Nazareth to thank Him for what He did for me, praise the Lord!"

Those present looked at him in astonishment, and Gedaliah and Manasseh's father confirmed this by saying, "Amen, my son."

Manasseh went on. "It is true that God makes me forget my affliction, just as it used to be with Joseph, the son of Jacob; for that is the meaning of Manasseh, my name: great is His Name and His deeds!"

The guests were surprised but nodded in agreement with this praise for the God of Israel.

But Manasseh was not finished yet and continued, "Luckily I was just in time. Jesus was already at the ship and was about to leave. I only had a moment to thank Him."

Then the party-goers devoured the meat of the slaughtered calf and drank cheerfully from the wine.

Source:
32. There some people brought to him a man who was deaf and could hardly talk, and they begged him to place his hand on the man.
33. After he took him aside, away from the crowd, Jesus put his fingers into the man's ears. Then he spit and touched the man's tongue.
34. He looked up to heaven and with a deep sigh said to him, "Ephphatha!" (which means, "Be opened!").
35. At this, the man's ears were opened, his tongue was loosened, and he began to speak plainly.
36. Jesus commanded them not to tell anyone. But the more he did so, the more they kept talking about it.
37. People were overwhelmed with amazement. "He has done everything well," they said. "He even makes the deaf hear and the mute speak." Mark 7 :32–37 (New International Version (NIV))

6.   Quintus Pedius, the Young Roman Painter

In the early morning, a shout of joy from the midwife sounded right through the walls of the Roman house. At last! What would it be? A son or a daughter?

Collicius, the slave of Quintus Pedius Publicola, thought, "It will be fine either way."

It was a son, who was born deaf and his name was Quintus Pedius.

The baby prospered. Collicius, who cared for him, had a problem. When the slave called him, the small one never listened.

Sometimes he was annoyed; his hands itched. However, he did realize that small toddlers were vulnerable. He did not want to make the same mistake as Corvinus, whose son was given such a beating in a fit of anger that the child became deaf.

Quintus was three years old and the annoyance of the slave remained. The small one was terribly stubborn and hardly ever listened. It was too much for Collicius; he wanted to grab the little boy to give him a thrashing, but then he heard Happaea, his mistress, say, "Wait, don't do that!"

"Lady, eh, I wasn't actually going to do that." But it was clear from the slave's face what his intentions had been. "Quintus did not listen and..."

"Yes, that's right. He can't hear. He is deaf. Yes. Servinus, the doctor, told me yesterday."

The slave bowed to the authority of the family doctor and sighed deeply. The mistress waited a moment and then walked from the room.

Collicius wondered whether the deafness of the little one could be his fault. He asked himself whether he had ever beaten him. No, he had never done that. Now he realized how terrible it must be for his master. What would he do with his little son? Would the child be thrown into the river Tiber because of his deafness? It was quite normal to throw a disabled child into the river as soon as the disability was discovered.

No, Collicius saw that Happaea's face was still and relaxed. Apparently, the deafness was no real problem for her and her husband.

One afternoon in August, Happaea told Collicius about Corvinus, the famous orator who was her uncle by marriage, and who also had a deaf son. The slave watched the mistress with open mouth and shook his head.

"What is it, Collicius?"

"Madam, I did know that Corvinus' son was also deaf, but I didn't know that you and he were related to each other."

Happaea laughed and asked her slave how he knew of the deafness of her cousin.

"My father, Atacinius Lerga," he replied.

After a short pause, Happaea said suddenly, "Collicius, I would like you to help me with Quintus' education."

He felt a strong inclination to say that such a thing was impossible. Then she quoted an orator unknown to him, who once said, "Nothing is impossible for those who want it…"

"Mistress, I will try."

"Sure, I get it. It will not be easy to educate my deaf son, but I'm counting on you."

"I will do my best," replied the slave, now a teacher.

Five years later Collicius woke up in a fright.

"Whoever shouted?" the old slave thought, annoyed.

The cry turned out to be from his master.

"Collicius, the emperor has just given his consent!"

"Permission Sir? To whom and what is this about?" the slave asked, confused.

Happaea also came into the room and laughed. Her face reflected an unspeakable happiness.

"The Emperor has allowed our son to take a painting course thanks to the intervention of Valerius Messalla Corvinus."

"What a great luck! Congratulations, Sir and Mistress," the slave said enthusiastically.

"Yes, thanks to our Quintus Pedius' grandmother."

"And I would ask you to follow me," commanded his master. However, the slave remained quiet, full of his thoughts.

"Come!"

"Yes, Sir. Forgive me."

In the room his master used to do part of the administration of the Roman Empire, the slave stood listening. He had even more to think about when he was subsequently told that from now on he would be allowed to live freely in thanks for his efforts. He would no longer be a slave!

After a while, Auclian Mucius asked, "What do you think you'll do now?"

"Master, this is such a surprise for me. Can I ask for a day of reflection?"

"You are allowed to do that," was the administrator's answer, and with that the wonderful conversation ended.

With some success, Quintus graduated from his painting course and so he became the first deaf person to be mentioned in Pliny the Elder's *Natural History*. However, it is not certain that he was deaf-born; the Latin words "natura mutus" (i.e. speechlessly born) are used in Pliny's text.

Source*:*
Mentioned in Book 35, Chapter 4 of Pliny the Elder's Natural History:
Pedius was the son of Roman Senator and orator Quintus Pedius Publicola, while his mother was an unnamed Roman woman. Pedius' paternal grandfather was the consul Quintus Pedius and his paternal grandmother was Valeria, a sister of Roman Senator and orator Marcus Valerius Messalla Corvinus. His paternal grandfather, Pedius, and Roman emperor, Augustus, were maternal second cousins (or first cousins once removed if Pedius was the son of Julia Major instead). Pedius was deaf-born. On the advice of his paternal great-uncle, Corvinus, and with permission from Augustus, Pedius was taught to paint.

The boy turned out to be a talented painter but died young. He is the first deaf person in history known by name; he was a noted painter of his time.

7.   The Nameless

"Look, there he is again," Des Tombes, the heavily built lord of the castle, complains. He has been a widower for several years, and his voice is unfriendly.

Aletta, his daughter, hears his harsh voice and immediately knows what her father is talking about. Nevertheless, she walks over to the window. And yes, there is the man in his shabby clothes on the other side of the wide moat. Because it is very hot, he is letting his muscular white legs and feet dangle in the water. Aletta, dressed in her fine riding dress, expresses her annoyance loudly. Marianne will be delighted by the presence of that nameless bum; that deaf and speechless vagabond.

After searching for a while in the various rooms of the castle, Aletta finds her eldest sister sitting at the spinning wheel in the weaving room.

"Marianne, o fairest maiden of the county, behold outside the handsomest of men!" Aletta says, with malicious sarcasm.

Looking up from her activities, her sister sighs. She could have known; it is always the same, year after year. When her sister leaves the room, she sneaks over to the window. She doesn't like it when Aletta interferes. When the Nameless sees Marianne, he waves energetically. She waves back like she has done in previous years. Aletta sees the man waving and is vexed by the whole thing. How silly of Marianne, waving to a bum. Who'd do such a thing? She feels hate for her sister, who is known for her uninhibited cordiality and willingness to help, regardless of class differences. She is much loved because of it. Aletta makes up her mind that this must stop.

Unlike her sister she feels strongly about her breeding and the distinction there must be between nobles and their servants. In the great hall, with many coats of arms covering the walls and armors in the corners, she hatches a devilish plot. Meditating, she stares while petting the falcon on her right arm gently.

The next morning, she initially shrinks back from her murderous plan, but soon her hate prevails, taking possession of her and intoxicating her. With a cruel smile she nods: the idea is good.

She makes up her mind to end matters quickly before that horrible tramp takes off again. Around noon she walks through the park at the edge of the river, taking her father's hunting dog with her. The falcon sways on her arms, clapping his wings occasionally. She finds the Nameless under a big tree.

Aletta is delighted to find he does not seem to have any intention of moving to another castle to collect a meal. She lets him pet Pollux, the dog, with unusual gentleness. Then she returns to the castle with the animals.

Sometime later, the Nameless, who possesses nothing, sees someone approaching with a knapsack in his hand. The person throws the bag in front of the Nameless and leaves hastily. With hesitation, the hungry wanderer picks it up and unties the knot. How wonderful! Fruit, a drumstick, and some bread. He eagerly eats everything, before anyone can take it from him again.

The next morning one of the servants makes a gruesome discovery. People come running at his screams to see Marianne's body lying at the door of the stables. Next to her lies an axe covered with blood and sand. The beloved maiden has been murdered. Her father arrives and his face turns pale as he sees his daughter lying dead. He covers his face with his hands and lets out a muffled cry.

Aletta, apparently just as shocked by the murder, embraces her father to comfort him. After some time, he raises his head, his cheeks turning purple with the anger that follows such loss.

"Who did this?" he asks with a trembling voice.

The servants cast down their eyes.

"Come on, tell me!"

He curses terribly. The servant responsible for the garden makes an attempt to speak but hesitates. The lord of the castle turns to him and his big hands take hold of the man's collar.

"Speak to me, what is it?"

"Well, I saw the lady Marianne…"

"You saw her? And? Did you kill her? I'll kill you too!"

Des Tombes' anger grows with each word he speaks. Then Aletta puts her hand on her father's arm and says, "Father, no, he hasn't done anything."

"Aletta? You know something about this?"

"It's just that I have my suspicions, but I cannot and will not express them here."

Her father nods and orders his servants to take Marianne's body to her bedroom.

"Daughter, follow me," he mumbles.

Aletta follows the broad figure of her father to his study. There she speaks with false passion of her suspicions about the killing of Marianne. Her father has no doubts and gives orders to track the killer.

A few hours later, the Nameless arrives at his usual spot in the park, underneath the big oak tree. To his surprise several sturdy men, servants of Des Tombes, approach him. Before he knows it, his wrists are tied together with a rope. His eyes wide with astonishment, he is led by the men to a dark cellar in the castle. Left alone, he wonders why he has been put in such a terrible place. With his tied hands, he bangs on the heavy door that separates him from his liberty.

The day after the funeral of the maiden, which attracts enormous crowds, the men take their prisoner to the courtyard.

Helplessly, the Nameless looks at Des Tombes, Aletta and the other residents of the castle. He feels how they hate and despise him. But why?

Aletta looks at him with a hidden smile, but she is startled when suddenly De Grasville, priest of the village, speaks out and pleads the innocence of the Nameless. Aletta wants to protest, but her father raises his hand.

"Let's hear what this man of God has to say."

"My lord, as far as I know, this man, for a man he is, is truly one of the meek. Others can tell you about his way with animals. He connects with them in a special, miraculous way."

Aletta moves restlessly. If only this stubborn priest would keep his pious mouth shut. But Des Tombes, who has great respect for De Grasville, responds to his objections.

He asks if anyone had actually seen the Nameless around the castle, or Marianne go to the stables.

Nobody had. He curses, feeling his need for revenge thwarted by his sense of justice. Aletta looks at him and notices the gray color of his skin. First his wife, now his favorite daughter: a bitter thought. She cannot bear to speak, and stares at him.

He looks at her and remembers her words. His daughter wouldn't lie. "Still, I have reason to believe this deaf-mute vagabond committed this terrible crime. I have seen how he was interested in Marianne; how he looked at her with those big eyes." Mumbling the last words, he points at the Nameless.

The priest steps forward but thinks better of it. Angering Des Tombes can be very dangerous, he knows. Even the Duke, the lord of the castle, fears him.

"Murder must be punished. This terrible act must be repaid. This man deserves to be hanged!"

The priest can no longer contain himself. "This is not a fair trial. There is no evidence!"

"But there is," Des Tombes replies and he looks at Aletta to make her repeat what she told her father before.

She had hoped to avoid attracting attention to her part in this, but she realizes it is too late for that. Des Tombes nods impatiently.

With an expressionless face, she says, "Surely this man had a part in the crime, Father. I saw him the day before yesterday on this courtyard, carrying an axe for no apparent reason."

"He helped me chop wood," a servant says, but only the people around him hear it.

Aletta notices the restlessness and repeats her last words: "No apparent reason."

Des Tombes turns toward the crowd and speaks with resolve. "The matter is closed. Tonight, we'll gather near the big oak in the park."

He orders some servants to ready the gallows. Delighted, Aletta withdraws. That afternoon she hears De Grasville enter the great hall to speak to her father. She hides behind one of the pillars and listens to the priest.

"Will you not reconsider? Are you really sentencing this innocent man?"

"Father, this vagabond, deaf and without speech, who does not even carry a name—what use does he have? Why does he even live?"

"Lord, I beg to differ. The Almighty, creator of heaven and earth, created this man as well, deaf and speechless as he is. God had his meaning with that."

For a while both men remain silent. The sun shines through the stained glass, projecting wonderful colors onto the gray floor.

"Are you sure, Father?"

"Completely," the priest replies.

Des Tombes sighs, and with chilling bitterness he says, "Well, tell me, Priest, if you are so sure, why do loved ones die, and so young at that? Did the Almighty have a meaning with that too?"

Aletta strains to hear the priest respond, but he doesn't speak. She hears the heavy footsteps of her father, and then a door closes with force.

The sun shines low through the leaves of the oak tree, and a crowd gathers around it. Most people look forward to the gruesome event that makes a welcome change to their dull lives, even though most of them liked the Nameless well enough.

Still tied up, the Nameless approaches the gallows, sees it, and suddenly realizes what is about to happen. He resists fiercely, but to no avail.

Standing below the noose, he tries to explain he did nothing, but he cannot sign with his hands tied behind his back and he never learned to speak. But everyone present can read the expression on his face of despair and deep indignation. The Nameless fixes his eyes on Aletta, and suddenly be understands she is the evil genius behind all this: that afternoon when she came to him, while he knew she despised him; the food— it was just to make sure he would be around. And Marianne? Where is she? He notices the black clothing of the members of the noble family and fully understands. His eyes fill with tears. She was a good woman, one of the few who did not reject him.

De Grasville, schooled to understand man, looks attentively at the Nameless.

"He knows more about it," he mutters. Then he sees Aletta stare back at the Nameless with a smug smile on her cold, pretty face. Carefully, De Grasville moves through the crowd until he reaches Aletta.

He whispers, "You must tell the truth or be forever damned!"

Aletta shrieks, frightened by his unexpected words.

Des Tombes turns to her. "My daughter, this is too much for you, I understand. Go and lie down while we settle this matter," he says unsuspectingly.

Aletta runs off, feeling nauseous with fear. De Grasville watches her flee and senses her guilt.

Des Tombes nods to the priest, who can do nothing but give the Nameless his final blessing, making the sign of the cross. His eyes speak of his pity for the man. The Nameless sees it, and smiles gently, to the amazement of the crowd. To the priest it is as if Christ on the cross smiles at him. Puzzled, he returns to his place, crossing himself repeatedly.

Des Tombes, angered by the smile which he ascribes to pure evil, shouts, "Set him on the stool."

Some men lift the Nameless and put him on the wobbly piece of furniture. With a noose around his neck, the Nameless trembles with fear and despairs again.

"Pollux!" the lord of the castle shouts.

Wagging his tail, the hunting dog runs to his master. Des Tombes puts a belt around its neck and attaches it to a leg of the stool. Des Tombes takes a few steps away from the dog, throws a piece of wood and then calls, "Pollux, fetch!"

The dog shoots away, obediently. The belt stretches and then the stool is jerked from underneath the Nameless' feet. The three-legged stool tumbles over on the grass as the dog comes to return the wood. The crowd laughs, but the priest watches the soulless body of the Nameless, dangling on the cord. Astonished and grieved, De Grasville covers his face with his hands. As he moves away from the scene, he sees Aletta approaching. She tries to avoid the cleric, but he goes up to her, staggering like an old man. She averts her eyes; he grabs her by her arms.

"This was wrong, Aletta; it is a sinful thing you have forced us to do. Murdering the
Nameless cannot avert God's curse from you and your father: don't think that it can!"

Terrified by these words she runs away. The next morning, she tells her father what the priest said.

"He said that? Well, well," Des Tombes laughs cynically. He then tells her what happened after she left, taking pleasure in describing all the details of the execution.

"We have nothing to fear. It was not I who executed the beggar, but my dear Pollux. And what a good job he did!"

8.   The Deafness of Ludwig van Beethoven

Despite the disadvantage of his limited hearing, Ludwig had incredible successes with composed music.

It's not surprising that his piano, which he had bought with his first earnings, started to exhibit signs of wear. That's what he thought at first when his fingers played on the keys on a beautiful spring day in 1798, and some of sounds of the piano seemed to drop away.

The next day, he arrived in the workplace of Johann Andreas Streicher and sat on the stool in front of a new piano.

"Streicher!" the celebrated pianist and composer called out.

Immediately, the piano manufacturer hurried toward Ludwig.

"What can I do for you, Sir?"

"This is a new piano? I cannot hear certain sounds!"

Streicher indicated that Ludwig's play sounded virtuoso as always and that he could certainly not hear a dissonant sound.

Ludwig thought it was curious but made an appointment for the tuning of his own piano. However, when the piano was tuned, it turned out that it was still in excellent condition.

After a period of confusion and uncertainty, Ludwig came to the conclusion that there might be something wrong with his hearing, and he decided to go to Liesl, his neighbor, to take a test. With great attention he listened to the girl's flute. He nodded, and Liesl heard him muttering now and then: "Stimmt…"

Later, he was at his wit's end. Despair took over him, and suddenly he realized what the ringing and rustling in his ears meant. He had always thought that there was too much music in his head, but now he realized with a shock that he was becoming deaf. He, the creator of extraordinary music according to music connoisseurs, would be deprived of his main tools.

Terrible! Disastrous! At the age of thirty, he was already condemned to beggary, and certain to be laughed at and mocked, just like the weird deaf man of the "Am Hof" Square.

From that moment onward, he consulted Wegeler, his friend and doctor, and secretly some other doctors. He did so in the hope that he could get his full hearing back. Instead, the deafness gradually worsened.

One of his surviving letters made clear Ludwig's state of mind. "My hearing has become weaker for three years now. My ears have been roaring and bubbling night and day. I may say that I had a miserable life for two years. I avoid any company, because I cannot say to people: 'I am deaf.'

"…to give you some understanding of this deafness, I can tell you that I have to sit in the theater near the orchestra to be able to follow the performance to some extent. I do not hear the instruments and the voices when I sit further away.

"…If this situation should continue, I will come to you in the coming spring, and you will have to rent a house for me in a beautiful spot. I will live there as a farmer for six months. Maybe that will do me well."

If you are ever walking through Vienna as a tourist, you'll pass the sign of the Vienna Tourist Information Office, which states, "In diesem Haus wohnte Beethoven…" [In this house, Beethoven lived]. According to Ates d'Arcy-Orga, in her book,

Beethoven: His Life and Times. Ludwig had a curious need to change rented rooms every six months and to change servants every six weeks. In the period 1815–1827, he changed his summer and winter residence thirty-one times. This caused a lot of annoyance and agitation to the people around him.

One day, he had to move again. In the end, he felt it was time to turn his back on Vienna. In 1802, he left for Heiligenstadt, which was close to Vienna. There he wrote what was later called "Heiligenstadter Testament" for his brothers, in which he put down everything that stirred his mind so violently and all his dejection and insecure feelings. The first words of this testament were:

"Oh, you people who hold me hostile and stern,

or see me as a man-hater, you are doing me

a wrong. You do not know the secret cause of mine…"

But when one day he realized that he could still read and write music, he was very pleased. From the time he was a child of about five years old, Ludwig learned to make music, and for more than twenty years he played the piano. He knew the sounds of the instruments inside out. During the last ten years he composed for orchestras. Would someone who becomes deaf, for example, at the age of twenty, be able to forget his mother tongue?

In any case, he decided to continue to devise and create new pieces of music. Now and then his mood changed and in a letter for his best friend he wrote:

"I will travel and, while playing the piano and composing,

I will suffer less; now I suffer the most, when I am among the people…"

In the year 1808, he once played on a church organ and suddenly he became aware of the strong vibrations that he felt in his body coming up through his feet. He sat petrified for minutes. All kinds of thoughts overwhelmed him, but in the end two things remained: he had his eyes and his feeling. He should make good use of them. Only, at home there was the problem that he absorbed the vibrations of the piano a lot less well. Ludwig solved this by using an ear horn so that he could catch some of the sounds.

Emil Ludwig wrote in his biography about Beethoven, "During a rehearsal of the Battle Symphony, Beethoven, as usual, gave a transition for a forte, but he did so ten bars too early. He turned around, he looked at the orchestra in astonishment, which continued to play pianissimo, and only composed himself when he heard the long-awaited forte!"

At this concert, the performance of the symphony would certainly have stalled at one point or another if bandleader Umlauf had not caught his baton, and had he not directed the orchestra behind Beethoven's back. When Beethoven finally sensed what was going on, a smile lit his face; "a heavenly smile," as an eyewitness recalls.

His hearing had completely disappeared by 1818. His ear horn became useless because of this.

There was an imperial school for the deaf in Vienna, but this offered little help to the deaf composer because the oral method was not taught at the time. They only used sign language.

And hearing people in those days often did not know how to communicate with a deaf person. Moreover, many people thought Beethoven to be a strange or crazy person. In addition, he paid very little attention to his appearance and his face was often a thundercloud. It was no wonder that people avoided his proximity. Ludwig had to use empty music notebooks and carpenter's pencils to make contact with people such as his few friends and business contacts. Like a sick animal, Ludwig often retired from the human community—he didn't want people to know about his deafness. Sometimes Ludwig walked through the countryside, and he would stop now and then, hoping, for example, to hear the whistle of a shepherd or the song of the birds, but it was always in vain. Ludwig was lucky that he still had his phenomenal memory, so he could easily play and improvise.

For almost thirty years he had to live with his deafness. The remarkable thing, however, is that it did not make him a beggar, but gave him great fame to this day.

9.　　Quasimodo and the Deaf Judge[1]

Number 39

"By Hercules! It's our prince of yesterday, our Pope of the Fools, our bell-ringer, our one-eyed man, our hunchback, our grimace! It's Quasimodo!"

It was he indeed.

It was Quasimodo, bound, corded, tied and garroted. The squad of men who had him in their charge were assisted by the captain of the watch in person, wearing the arms of France embroidered on his breast and the city arms on his back. There was nothing, however, about Quasimodo, except his deformity, that could justify this display of halberds and harquebuses; he was gloomy, silent, and quiet. His solitary eye merely cast an occasional crafty, angry glance at the bonds which held him.

He gazed about him with the same expression, but he looked so dull and sleepy that the women only pointed him out to each other to mock at him.

Meanwhile, the judge, Master Florian, was attentively browsing the documents relating to the complaint filed against Quasimodo, and he seemed to think for a moment. He always took the time before starting an interrogation and so he knew in advance what the names, occupation, and crimes of the criminals were. That way, nobody knew about his deafness, as he thought it best to keep

---

[1] *The Hunchback of Notre-Dame by Victor Hugo (1831). Translated by Isabel F. Hapgood in 1888 from the French Book VI Chapter 1.*

it a secret. After Master Florian had studied Quasimodo's case, he leaned back and half-closed his eyes, his hand relaxed on his right cheek.

That way he tried to create the atmosphere of the ceremony and invoke his impartiality so that he was deaf and blind at the same time. With that magisterial attitude, he started an interrogation.

"Your name?"

Now, here was a case which had not been "provided for by the law"—that of one deaf man questioning another.

Quasimodo, quite unaware of the question, continued to gaze fixedly at the judge and did not answer. The judge, deaf, and wholly unaware of the prisoner's deafness, supposed that he had answered, as all prisoners were wont to do, and went on, with his mechanical and stupid self-assurance.

"Good! Your age?"

Quasimodo made no answer. The judge was satisfied and continued.

"Now, your business?"

Still the same silence. The audience began to whisper and look at each other.

"That will do," resumed the imperturbable judge, when he supposed that the prisoner had ended his third answer. "You are accused, before us, primo, of making a nocturnal disturbance; secondo, of an indecent assault upon the person of a woman of easy virtue, in projudicium meretricis; tertio, of rebellion and disloyalty toward the archers of the guard of our lord the king. What have you to say for yourself on all these points? Clerks, have you written down all that the prisoner has said thus far?"

At this unfortunate question a shout of laughter burst from both clerk and audience, so violent, so hearty, so contagious, so universal, that even the two deaf men could not fail to notice it. Quasimodo turned away, shrugging his hump in disdain, while Master Florian, equally surprised, and supposing the laughter of the spectators to be provoked by some irreverent reply from the prisoner, made apparent to him by that shrug, addressed him most indignantly.

"Such an answer like that, you rascal, deserves the halter! Do you know to whom you speak?"

This outburst was scarcely adapted to silence the sounds of merriment. It seemed to all so absurd and ridiculous that the contagious laughter spread to the very sergeants from the Commonalty Hall, the kind of men-at-arms whose stupidity is their uniform. Quasimodo alone preserved his gravity, for the very good reason that he understood nothing of what was going on around him. The judge, more and more indignant, felt obliged to proceed in the same strain, hoping in this way to strike the prisoner with a terror which would react upon the audience and restore them to a due sense of respect for him.

"So then, perverse and thievish knave, you venture to insult the judge of the Chatelet, the chief magistrate of the police courts of Paris, appointed to inquire into all crimes, offences, and misdemeanors; to control all trades and prevent monopoly; to keep the pavements in repair; to put down hucksters of poultry, fowl, and game; to superintend the measuring of logs and firewood; to cleanse the city of mud and the air of contagious diseases in a word, to watch continually over the public welfare, without wages or hope of salary!

"Do you know that my name is Florian Barbedienne, and that I am the Lord Provost's own deputy, and, moreover, commissary, comptroller, and examiner with equal power in provost, bailiwick, court of registration, and presidia court?"

There is no reason why a deaf man talking to a deaf man should ever cease talking. Heaven knows when Master Florian, thus launched on the full flood of his own eloquence, would have paused if the low door at the back of the room had not suddenly opened and admitted the provost himself.

At his entrance Master Florian did not stop short but, turning half round on his heel and abruptly subjecting the provost to the harangue with which but a moment before he had been overwhelming Quasimodo, he said: "My lord, I demand such sentence as it may please you to inflict upon the prisoner here present, for his grave and heinous contempt of court."

And he sat down again quite out of breath, wiping away the big beads of moisture which ran down his face like tears, wetting the papers spread out before him.

Master Robert d'Estouteville frowned and commanded Quasimodo's attention by a sign so imperious and significant that even the deaf man understood something of his meaning.

The provost addressed him severely: "What brings you here, scoundrel?"

The poor wretch, supposing that the provost asked his name, broke his habitual silence, and answered in a hoarse and guttural voice, "Quasimodo."

The answer had so little to do with the question that an irresistible laugh ran around the room again, and Master Robert cried out, red with rage, "Would you mock me too, your arrant knave?"

"Bell-ringer of Notre-Dame," replied Quasimodo, fancying himself called upon to explain to the provost who he was.

"Bell-ringer, indeed!" responded the provost, who, as we have already said, had woken in an ill enough humor that morning not to require any fanning of the flames of his fury by such strange answers. "Bell-ringer! I'll have a peal of switches rung upon your back through all the streets of Paris! Do you hear me, rascal?"

Number 40

"If you want to know my age," said Quasimodo, "I believe I shall be twenty on Saint Martin's Day."

This was too much; the provost could bear it no longer.

"Oh, you defy the provost's office, do you, wretch?! Vergers, take this scamp to the pillory in the Place de Grève; beat him well, and then turn him for an hour. He shall pay me for this, tête-Dieu! And I order this sentence to be proclaimed, by the aid of your sworn trumpeters, throughout the seven castellanies of the jurisdiction of Paris."

The clerk wrote down the sentence at once.

"A wise sentence, by God!" exclaimed the little student, Jehan Frollo du Moulin, from his corner.

The provost turned, and again fixed his flashing eyes upon Quasimodo: "I believe the scamp said, 'By God!' Clerk, add a fine of twelve Paris pence for swearing, and let half of it go to the Church of Saint Eustache; I am particularly fond of Saint Eustache."

In a few moments, the sentence was drawn up. It was simple and brief in tenor.

The common law of the provost and viscount of Paris had not yet been elaborated by the president, Thibaut Baillet, and by Roger Barmue, the king's advocate; it was not then obscured by that mass of quirks and quibbles which these two lawyers introduced at the beginning of the sixteenth century.

Everything about it was clear, expeditious, and explicit. It went straight to the mark, and at the end of every path, unconcealed by brambles or briers, the wheel, the gallows, or the pillory could plainly be seen from the very outset. At least you knew what was coming.

The clerk handed the sentence to the provost, who affixed his seal to it, and left the room to continue his round of the courts, in a state of mind which must have added largely that day to the population of the jails of Paris. Jehan Frollo and Robin Poussepain laughed in their sleeves. Quasimodo looked on with indifference.

But the clerk, just as Master Florian Barbedienne was reading the sentence in his turn before signing it, felt a twinge of pity for the poor devil of a prisoner, and in the hopes of gaining some lessening of his punishment, leaned as close as he could to the judge's ear, and said, pointing to Quasimodo, "That fellow is deaf."

He hoped that their common infirmity might rouse Master Florian's interest in the prisoner's favor. But, in the first place, we have already observed that Master Florian did not care to have his deafness noticed. Also, he was so hard of hearing that he caught not one word of what the clerk said to him; and yet, he wanted to have it appear that he heard, and therefore answered. "Oho! That's a different matter; I did not know that. Give him another hour in the pillory, in that case."

And he signed the sentence with this modification.

"Well done!" said Robin Poussepain, who bore Quasimodo a grudge. "That will teach him to maltreat folks."

10.   Mumu[2]

In one of the outlying streets of Moscow, in a gray house with white columns and a balcony, warped all askew, there was once living a lady, a widow, surrounded by a numerous household of serfs. Her sons were in the government service at Petersburg; her daughters were married; she went out very little, and in solitude lived through the last years of her miserly and dreary old age. Her day, a joyless and gloomy day, had long been over; but the evening of her life was blacker than night.

Of all her servants, the most remarkable personage was the porter, Gerasim, a man full twelve inches over the normal height, of heroic build, and deaf and dumb from his birth. The lady, his owner, had brought him up from the village where he lived alone in a little hut, apart from his brothers, and was reckoned about the most punctual of her peasants in the payment of the seignorial dues.

Endowed with extraordinary strength, he did the work of four men; work flew apace under his hands, and it was a pleasant sight to see him when he was ploughing, while, with his huge palms pressing hard upon the plough, he seemed alone, unaided by his poor horse, to cleave the yielding bosom of the earth, or when, about St. Peter's Day, he plied his scythe with a furious energy that might have mown a young birch copse up by the roots, or swiftly and untiringly wielded a flail over two yards long; while the hard

[2] *Mumu by Ivan Turgenev, 1852, originally published in 1854. Translation by Constance Clara Garnett (1861–1946), published in 1898*

oblong muscles of his shoulders rose and fell like a lever. His perpetual silence lent a solemn dignity to his un wearying labor. He was a splendid peasant, and, except for his affliction, any girl would have been glad to marry him...

But now they had taken Gerasim to Moscow, bought him boots, had him made a full-skirted coat for summer, a sheepskin for winter, put into his hand a broom and a spade, and appointed him porter.

At first, he intensely disliked his new mode of life. From his childhood he had been used to field labor, to village life. Shut off by his affliction from the society, of men, he had grown up, dumb and mighty, as a tree grows on a fruitful soil. When he was transported to the town, he could not understand what was being done with him; he was miserable and stupefied, with the stupefaction of some strong young bull, taken straight from the meadow, where the rich grass stood up to his belly, taken and put in the truck of a railway train, and there, while smoke and sparks and gusts of steam puff out upon the sturdy beast, he is whirled onwards, whirled along with loud roar and whistle, whither—God knows!

What Gerasim had to do in his new duties seemed a mere trifle to him after his hard toil as a peasant; in half an hour all his work was done, and he would once more stand stock-still in the middle of the courtyard, staring open-mouthed at all the passers-by, as though trying to wrest from them the explanation of his perplexing position; or he would suddenly go off into some corner, and flinging a long way off the broom or the spade, throw himself on his face on the ground, and lie for hours together without stirring, like a caged beast.

But man gets used to anything, and Gerasim got used at last to living in town. He had little work to do; his whole duty consisted in keeping the courtyard clean, bringing in a barrel of water twice a day, splitting and dragging in wood for the kitchen and the house, keeping out strangers, and watching at night. And it must be said he did his duty zealously. In his courtyard there was never a shaving lying about, never a speck of dust; if sometimes, in the muddy season, the wretched nag, put under his charge for fetching water, got stuck in the road, he would simply give it a shove with his shoulder, and set not only the cart but the horse itself moving.

If he set to chopping wood, the axe fairly rang like glass, and chips and chunks flew in all directions. And as for strangers, after he had one night caught two thieves and knocked their heads together—knocked them so that there was not the slightest need to take them to the police-station afterwards—everyone in the neighborhood began to feel a great respect for him; even those who came in the daytime, by no means robbers, but simply unknown persons, at the sight of the terrible porter, waved and shouted to him as though he could hear their shouts.

With all the rest of the servants, Gerasim was on terms hardly friendly—they were afraid of him but familiar; he regarded them as his fellows. They explained themselves to him by signs, and he understood them, and exactly carried out all orders, but knew his own rights too, and soon no one dared to take his seat at the table. Gerasim was altogether of a strict and serious temper, he liked order in everything; even the cocks did not dare to fight in his presence, or woe betides them!

Directly he caught sight of them, he would seize them by the legs, swing them ten times around in the air like a wheel, and throw them in different directions. There were geese, too, kept in the yard; but the goose, as is well known, is a dignified and reasonable bird: Gerasim felt a respect for them, looked after them, and fed them; he was himself not unlike a gander of the steppes. He was assigned a little garret over the kitchen; he arranged it himself to his own liking, made a bedstead in it of oak boards on four stumps of wood for legs a truly bedstead; one might have put a ton or two on it would not have bent under the load; under the bed was a solid chest; in a corner stood a little table of the same strong kind, and near the table a three-legged stool, so solid and squat that Gerasim himself would sometimes pick it up and drop it again with a smile of delight. The garret was locked up by means of a padlock that looked like a kalatch or basket-shaped loaf, only black; the key of this padlock Gerasim always carried about him in his girdle. He did not like people to come to his garret.

So, passed a year, at the end of which a little incident befell Gerasim.

The old lady, in whose service he lived as porter, adhered in everything to the ancient ways, and kept a large number of servants. In her house were not only laundresses, sempstresses, carpenters, tailors and tailoresses, there was even a harness-maker—he was reckoned as a veterinary surgeon, too, and a doctor for the servants; there was a household doctor for the mistress; there was, lastly, a shoemaker, by name Kapiton Klimov, a sad drunkard. Klimov regarded himself as an injured creature, whose merits were unappreciated, a cultivated man from Petersburg, who ought not to be living in Moscow without occupation—in the wilds, so to speak; and if he drank, as he himself expressed it emphatically, with a blow on his chest, it was sorrow drove him to it.

So, one day his mistress had a conversation about him with her head steward, Gavrila, a man whom, judging solely from his little yellow eyes and nose like a duck's beak, fate itself, it seemed, had marked out as a person in authority. The lady expressed her regret at the corruption of the morals of Kapiton, who had, only the evening before, been picked up somewhere in the street.

"Now, Gavrila," she observed, all of a sudden, "now, if we were to marry him, what do you think, perhaps he would be steadier?"

"Why not marry him, indeed, 'm? He could be married, 'm," answered Gavrila, "and it would be a very good thing, to be sure, 'm."

"Yes; only who is to marry him?"

"Ay, 'm. But that's at your pleasure, 'm. He may, anyway, so to say, be wanted for something; he can't be turned adrift altogether."

"I fancy he likes Tatiana."

Gavrila was on the point of making some reply, but he shut his lips tightly.

"Yes!... let him marry Tatiana," the lady decided, taking a pinch of snuff complacently, "Do you hear?"

"Yes, 'm," Gavrila articulated, and he withdrew.

Returning to his room (it was in a little lodge and was almost filled up with metal-bound trunks), Gavrila first sent his wife away, and then sat down at the window and pondered. His mistress's unexpected arrangement had clearly put him in a difficulty. At last he got up and sent to call Kapiton. Kapiton made his appearance... But before reporting their conversation to the reader, we consider it not out of place to relate in few words who was this Tatiana, whom it was to be Kapiton's lot to marry, and why the great lady's order had disturbed the steward.

Tatiana, one of the laundresses referred to above (as a trained and skillful laundress she was in charge of the fine linen only), was a woman of twenty-eight, thin, fair-haired, with moles on her left cheek. Moles on the left cheek are regarded as of evil omen in Russia a token of unhappy life... Tatiana could not boast of her good luck.

From her earliest youth she had been badly treated; she had done the work of two and had never known affection; she had been poorly clothed and had received the smallest wages. Relations she had practically none; an uncle she had once had, a butler, left behind in the country as useless, and other uncles of hers were peasants that was all. At one time she had passed for a beauty, but her good looks were very soon over. In disposition, she was very meek, or, rather, scared; towards herself, she felt perfect indifference; of others, she stood in mortal dread; she thought of nothing but how to get her work done in good time, never talked to anyone, and trembled at the very name of her mistress, though the latter scarcely knew her by sight.

When Gerasim was brought from the country, she was ready to die with fear on seeing his huge figure, tried all she could to avoid meeting him, even dropped her eyelids when sometimes she chanced to run past him, hurrying from the house to the laundry.

Gerasim at first paid no special attention to her, then he used to smile when she came his way, then he began even to stare admiringly at her, and at last he never took his eyes off her. She took his fancy, whether by the mild expression of her face or the timidity of her movements, who can tell?

So, one day she was stealing across the yard, with a starched dressing-jacket of her mistresses carefully poised on her outspread fingers... someone suddenly grasped her vigorously by the elbow; she turned around and fairly screamed; behind her stood Gerasim. With a foolish smile, making inarticulate caressing grunts, he held out to her a gingerbread cock with gold tinsel on his tail and wings. She was about to refuse it, but he thrust it forcibly into her hand, shook his head, walked away, and turning around, once more grunted something very affectionately to her.

From that day forward, he gave her no peace; wherever she went, he was on the spot at once, coming to meet her, smiling, grunting, waving his hands; all at once he would pull a ribbon out of the bosom of his smock and put it in her hand, or would sweep the dust out of her way.

The poor girl simply did not know how to behave or what to do. Soon the whole household knew of the dumb porter's wiles; jeers, jokes, sly hints, were showered upon Tatiana. At Gerasim, however, it was not everyone who would dare to scoff; he did not like jokes; indeed, in his presence, she, too, was left in peace. Whether she liked it or not, the girl found herself to be under his protection.

Like all deaf-mutes, he was very suspicious, and very readily perceived when they were laughing at him or at her. One day, at dinner, the wardrobe-keeper, Tatiana's superior, fell to nagging, as it is called, at her, and brought the poor thing to such a state that she did not know where to look, and was almost crying with vexation.

Gerasim got up all of a sudden, stretched out his gigantic hand, laid it on the wardrobe-maid's head, and looked into her face with such grim ferocity that her head positively flopped upon the table. Everyone was still.
Gerasim took up his spoon again and went on with his cabbage-soup.

"Look at him, the dumb devil, the wood-demon!" they all muttered in undertones, while the wardrobe-maid got up and went out into the maid's room.

Another time, noticing that Kapiton the same Kapiton who was the subject of the conversation reported above was gossiping somewhat too attentively with Tatiana, Gerasim beckoned him to him, led him into the cart shed, and taking up a shaft that was standing in a corner by one end, lightly, but most significantly, menaced him with it. Since then no one addressed a word to Tatiana.

And all this cost him nothing. It is true the wardrobe-maid, as soon as she reached the maids' room, promptly fell into a fainting fit, and behaved altogether so skillfully that Gerasim's rough action reached his mistress's knowledge the same day. But the capricious old lady only laughed, and several times, to the great offence of the wardrobe-maid, forced her to repeat "how he bent your head down with his heavy hand," and next day she sent Gerasim a roble.

She looked on him with favor as a strong and faithful watchman. Gerasim stood in considerable awe of her, but, all the same, he had hopes of her favor, and was preparing to go to her with a petition for leave to marry Tatiana.

He was only waiting for a new coat, promised him by the steward, to present a proper appearance before his mistress, when this same mistress suddenly took it into her head to marry Tatiana to Kapiton.

The reader will now readily understand the perturbation of mind that overtook the steward Gavrila after his conversation with his mistress. "My lady," he thought, as he sat at the window, "favors Gerasim, to be sure."

(Gavrila was well aware of this, and that was why he himself looked on him with an indulgent eye)—"still he is a speechless creature. I could not, indeed, put it before the mistress that Gerasim's courting Tatiana. But, after all, it's true enough; he's a queer sort of husband. But on the other hand, that devil, God forgive me, has only got to find out they're marrying Tatiana to Kapiton, he'll smash up everything in the house, 'pon my soul! There's no reasoning with him; why, he's such a devil, God forgive my sins, there's no getting over him no how... 'pon my soul!"

Kapiton's entrance broke the thread of Gavrila's reflections. The dissipated shoemaker came in, his hands behind him, and lounging carelessly against a projecting angle of the wall, near the door, crossed his right foot in front of his left, and tossed his head, as much as to say, "What do you want?"

Gavrila looked at Kapiton and drummed with his fingers on the window-frame. Kapiton merely screwed up his leaden eyes a little, but he did not look down; he even grinned slightly and passed his hand over his whitish locks which were sticking up in all directions. "Well, here I am. What is it?"

"You're a pretty fellow," said Gavrila, and paused. "A pretty fellow you are, there's no denying!"

Kapiton only twitched his little shoulders. "Are you any better, pray?" he thought to himself.

"Just look at yourself, now, look at yourself," Gavrila went on reproachfully; "now, whatever do you look like?"

Kapiton serenely surveyed his shabby, tattered coat and his patched trousers, and with special attention stared at his burst boots, especially the one on the tiptoe of which his right foot so gracefully poised, and he fixed his eyes again on the steward.

"Well?"

"Well?" repeated Gavrila. "Well? And then you say well? You look like Old Nick himself, God forgive my saying so, that's what you look like."

Kapiton blinked rapidly.

"Go on abusing me, go on, if you like, Gavrila Andreitch," he thought to himself again.

"Here you've been drunk again," Gavrila began, "drunk again, haven't you? Eh? Come, answer me!"

"Owing to the weakness of my health, I have exposed myself to spirituous beverages, certainly," replied Kapiton.

"Owing to the weakness of your health!... They let you off too easy, that's what it is; and you've been apprenticed in Petersburg... Much you learned in your apprenticeship! You simply eat your bread in idleness."

"In that matter, Gavrila Andreitch, there is One to judge me, the Lord God Himself, and no one else. He also knows what manner of man I be in this world, and whether I eat my bread in idleness. And as concerning your contention regarding drunkenness, in that matter, too, I am not to blame, but rather a friend; he led me into temptation, but was diplomatic and got away, while I..."

"While you were left like a goose, in the street. Ah, you're a dissolute fellow! But that's not the point," the steward went on, "I've something to tell you. Our lady..." here he paused a minute, "it's our lady's pleasure that you should be married. Do you hear? She imagines you may be steadier when you're married. Do you understand?"

"To be sure I do."

"Well, then. For my part I think it would be better to give you a good hiding. But there—it's her business. Well? are you agreeable?"

Kapiton grinned.

"Matrimony is an excellent thing for any one, Gavrila Andreitch; and, as far as I am concerned, I shall be quite agreeable."

"Very well, then," replied Gavrila, while he reflected to himself: "There's no denying the man expresses himself very properly. Only there's one thing," he pursued aloud: "the wife our lady' s picked out for you is an unlucky choice."

"Why, who is she, permit me to inquire?"

"Tatiana."

"Tatiana?"

And Kapiton opened his eyes and moved a little away from the wall.

"Well, what are you in such a taking for?... Isn't she to your taste, hey?"

"Not to my taste, do you say, Gavrila Andreitch? She's right enough, a hard-working steady girl... But you know very well yourself, Gavrila Andreitch, why that fellow, that wild man of the woods, that monster of the steppes, he's after her, you know..."

"I know, mate, I know all about it," the butler cut him short in a tone of annoyance: "but there, you see..."

"But upon my soul, Gavrila Andreitch! why, he'll kill me, by God, he will, he'll crush me like some fly; why, he's got a fist—why, you kindly look yourself what a fist he's got; why, he's simply got a fist like Minin Pozharsky's. You see he's deaf, he beats and does not hear how he's beating! He swings his great fists, as if he's asleep. And there's no possibility of pacifying him; and for why? Why, because, as you know yourself, Gavrila Andreitch, he's deaf, and what's more, has no more wit than the heel of my foot. Why, he's a sort of beast, a heathen idol, Gavrila Andreitch, and worse... a block of wood; what have I done that I should have to suffer from him now? Sure, it is, it's all over me now; I've knocked about, I've had enough to put up with, I've been battered like an earthenware pot, but still I'm a man, after all, and not a worthless pot."

"I know, I know, don't go talking away..."

"Lord, my God!" the shoemaker continued warmly, "when is the end? when, O Lord! A poor wretch I am, a poor wretch whose sufferings are endless!

What a life, what a life mine's been come to think of it! In my young days, I was beaten by a German I was 'prentice to; in the prime of life beaten by my own countrymen, and last of all, in ripe years, see what I have been brought to."

"Ugh, your flabby soul!" said Gavrila Andreitch. "Why do you make so many words about it?"

"Why, do you say, Gavrila Andreitch? It's not a beating I'm afraid of, Gavrila Andreitch. A gentleman may chastise me in private, but give me a civil word before folks, and I'm a man still; but see now, whom I've to do with..."

"Come, get along," Gavrila interposed impatiently. Kapiton turned away and staggered off.

"But, if it were not for him," the steward shouted after him, "you would consent for your part?"

"I signify my acquiescence," retorted Kapiton as he disappeared.

His fine language did not desert him, even in the most trying positions.

The steward walked several times up and down the room.

"Well, call Tatiana now," he said at last.

A few instants later, Tatiana had come up almost noiselessly, and was standing in the doorway.

"What are your orders, Gavrila Andreitch?" she said in a soft voice.

The steward looked at her intently.

"Well, Taniusha," he said, "would you like to be married? Our lady has chosen a husband for you?"

"Yes, Gavrila Andreitch. And whom has she deigned to name as a husband for me?" she added falteringly.

"Kapiton, the shoemaker."

"Yes, sir."

"He's a feather-brained fellow, that's certain. But it's just for that the mistress reckons upon you."

"Yes, sir."

"There's one difficulty... you know the deaf man, Gerasim, he's courting you, you see. How did you come to bewitch such a bear? But you see, he'll kill you, very like, he's such a bear..."

"He'll kill me, Gavrila Andreitch, he'll kill me, and no mistake."

"Kill you... Well we shall see about that. What do you mean by saying he'll kill you? Has he any right to kill you? tell me yourself."

"I don't know, Gavrila Andreitch, about his having any right or not."

"What a woman! Why, you've made him no promise, I suppose..."

"What are you pleased to ask of me?"

The steward was silent for a little, thinking, "You're a meek soul! Well, that's right," he said aloud; "we'll have another talk with you later, now you can go, Taniusha; I see you're not unruly, certainly."

Tatiana turned, steadied herself a little against the doorpost, and went away.

"And, perhaps, our lady will forget all about this wedding by to-morrow," thought the steward; "and here am I worrying myself for nothing! As for that insolent fellow, we must tie him down if it comes to that, we must let the police know... Ustinya Fyedorovna!" he shouted in a loud voice to his wife, "heat the samovar, my good soul..."

All that day Tatiana hardly went out of the laundry. At first, she had started crying, then she wiped away her tears, and set to work as before. Kapiton stayed till late at night at the gin-shop with a friend of his, a man of gloomy appearance, to whom he related in detail how he used to live in Petersburg with a gentleman, who would have been all right, except he was a bit too strict, and he had a slight weakness besides, he was too fond of drink; and, as to the fair sex, he didn't stick at anything.

His gloomy companion merely said yes; but when Kapiton announced at last that, in a certain event, he would have to lay hands on himself to-morrow, his gloomy companion remarked that it was bedtime. And they parted in surly silence.

Meanwhile, the steward's anticipations were not fulfilled.

The old lady was so much taken up with the idea of Kapiton's wedding, that even in the night she talked of nothing else to one of her companions, who was kept in her house solely to entertain her in case of sleeplessness, and, like a night cabman, slept in the day.

When Gavrila came to her after morning tea with his report, her first question was: "And how about our wedding is it getting on all right?" He replied, of course, that it was getting on first-rate, and that Kapiton would appear before her to pay his reverence to her that day.

The old lady was not quite well; she did not give much time to business. The steward went back to his own room and called a council. The matter certainly called for serious consideration. Tatiana would make no difficulty, of course; but Kapiton had declared in the hearing of all that he had but one head to lose, not two or three...

Gerasim turned rapid sullen looks on every one, would not budge from the steps of the maids' quarters, and seemed to guess that some mischief was being hatched against him. They met together. Among them was an old sideboard waiter, nicknamed Uncle Tail, to whom everyone looked respectfully for counsel, though all they got out of him was, "Here's a pretty pass! to be sure, to be sure, to be sure!"

As a preliminary measure of security, to provide against contingencies, they locked Kapiton up in the lumber-room where the filter was kept; then considered the question with the gravest deliberation. It would, to be sure, be easy to have recourse to force. But Heaven save us! There would be an uproar, the mistress would be put out—it would be awful! What should they do?

They thought and thought, and at last thought out a solution. It had many a time been observed that Gerasim could not bear drunkards... As he sat at the gates, he would always turn away with disgust when someone passed by intoxicated, with unsteady steps and his cap on one side of his ear. They resolved that Tatiana should be instructed to pretend to be tipsy and should pass by Gerasim staggering and reeling about.

The poor girl refused for a long while to agree to this, but they persuaded her at last; she saw, too, that it was the only possible way of getting rid of her adorer. She went out. Kapiton was released from the lumber-room; for, after all, he had an interest in the affair.

Gerasim was sitting on the curbstone at the gates, scraping the ground with a spade... From behind every corner, from behind every window-blind, the others were watching him... The trick succeeded beyond all expectations. On seeing Tatiana, at first, he nodded as usual, making caressing, inarticulate sounds; then he looked carefully at her, dropped his spade, jumped up, went up to her, brought his face close to her face... In her fright she staggered more than ever, and shut her eyes...

He took her by the arm, whirled her right across the yard, and going into the room where the council had been sitting, pushed her straight at Kapiton. Tatiana fairly swooned away... Gerasim stood, looked at her, waved his hand, laughed, and went off, stepping heavily, to his garret... For the next twenty-four hours he did not come out of it.

The postilion Antipka said afterwards that he saw Gerasim through a crack in the wall, sitting on his bedstead, his face in his hand. From time to time he uttered soft regular sounds; he was wailing a dirge, that is, swaying backwards and forwards with his eyes shut, and shaking his head as drivers or bargemen do when they chant their melancholy songs. Antipka could not bear it, and he came away from the crack.

When Gerasim came out of the garret next day, no particular change could be observed in him.
He only seemed, as it were, more morose, and took not the slightest notice of Tatiana or Kapiton. The same evening, they both had to

appear before their mistress with geese under their arms, and in a week's time they were married.

Even on the day of the wedding Gerasim showed no change of any sort in his behavior. Only, he came back from the river without water, he had somehow broken the barrel on the road; and at night, in the stable, he washed and rubbed down his horse so vigorously, it swayed like a blade of grass in the wind and staggered from one leg to the other under his fists of iron.

All this had taken place in the spring. Another year passed by, during which Kapiton became a hopeless drunkard, and as being absolutely of no use for anything, was sent away with the store wagons to a distant village with his wife.
On the day of his departure, he put a very good face on it at first, and declared that he would always be at home, send him where they would, even to the other end of the world; but later on, he lost heart, began grumbling that he was being taken to uneducated people, and collapsed so completely at last that he could not even put his own hat on. Some charitable soul stuck it on his forehead, set the peak straight in front, and thrust it on with a slap from above.

When everything was quite ready, and the peasants already held the reins in their hands and were only waiting for the words "With God's blessing!" to start, Gerasim came out of his garret, went up to Tatiana, and gave her as a parting present a red cotton handkerchief he had bought for her a year ago. Tatiana, who had up to that instant borne all the revolting details of her life with great indifference, could not control herself upon that; she burst into tears, and as she took her seat in the cart, she kissed Gerasim three times like a good Christian.

He meant to accompany her as far as the town-barrier, and did walk beside her cart for a while, but he stopped suddenly at the Crimean ford, waved his hand, and walked away along the riverside.

It was getting towards evening. He walked slowly, watching the water. All of a sudden, he fancied something was floundering in the mud close to the bank. He stooped over and saw a little white-and-black puppy, who, in spite of all its efforts, could not get out of the water; it was struggling, slipping back, and trembling all over its thin wet little body.

Gerasim looked at the unlucky little dog, picked it up with one hand, put it into the bosom of his coat, and hurried with long steps homewards. He went into his garret, put the rescued puppy on his bed, covered it with his thick overcoat, ran first to the stable for straw, and then to the kitchen for a cup of milk.

Carefully folding back, the overcoat, and spreading out the straw, he set the milk on the bedstead. The poor little puppy was not more than three weeks old, its eyes were just open—one eye still seemed rather larger than the other; it did not know how to lap out of a cup and did nothing but shiver and blink.

Gerasim took hold of its head softly with two fingers and dipped its little nose into the milk. The pup suddenly began lapping greedily, sniffing, shaking itself, and choking.

Gerasim watched and watched it, and all at once he laughed outright... All night long he was waiting on it, keeping it covered, and rubbing it dry. He fell asleep himself at last and slept quietly and happily by its side.

No mother could have looked after her baby as Gerasim looked after his little nursling. At first, she for the pup turned out to be a bitch was very weak, feeble, and ugly, but by degrees she grew stronger and improved in looks, and, thanks to the unflagging care of her preserver, in eight months' time she was transformed into a very pretty dog of the spaniel breed, with long ears, a bushy spiral tail, and large, expressive eyes.

She was devotedly attached to Gerasim and was never a yard from his side; she always followed him about wagging her tail.

He had even given her a name the dumb know that their inarticulate noises call the attention of others. He called her Mumu. All the servants in the house liked her, and called her Mumu, too. She was very intelligent, she was friendly with everyone, but was only fond of Gerasim.

Gerasim, on his side, loved her passionately, and he did not like it when other people stroked her; whether he was afraid for her, or jealous—God knows!

She used to wake him in the morning, pulling at his coat; she used to take the reins in her mouth, and bring him up the old horse that carried the water, with whom she was on very friendly terms.

With a face of great importance, she used to go with him to the river; she used to watch his brooms and spades, and never allowed anyone to go into his garret. He cut a little hole in his door on purpose for her, and she seemed to feel that only in Gerasim's garret she was completely mistress and at home; and directly she went in, she used to jump with a satisfied air upon the bed.

At night she did not sleep at all, but she never barked without sufficient cause, like some stupid house-dog, who, sitting on its hind-legs, blinking, with its nose in the air, barks simply from dullness, at the stars, usually three times in succession.

No! Mumu's delicate little voice was never raised without good reason; either some stranger was passing close to the fence, or there was some suspicious sound or rustle somewhere... In fact, she was an excellent watch-dog.

It is true that there was another dog in the yard, a tawny old dog with brown spots, called Wolf, but he was never, even at night, let off the chain; and, indeed, he was so decrepit that he did not even wish for freedom.

He used to lie curled up in his kennel, and only rarely uttered a sleepy, almost noiseless bark, which broke off at once, as though he were himself aware of its uselessness.

Mumu never went into the mistress's house; and when Gerasim carried wood into the rooms, she always stayed behind, impatiently waiting for him at the steps, pricking up her ears and turning her head to right and to left at the slightest creak of the door...

So, passed another year. Gerasim went on performing his duties as house-porter, and was very well content with his lot, when suddenly an unexpected incident occurred... One fine summer day the old lady was walking up and down the drawing-room with her dependants. She was in high spirits; she laughed and made jokes.

Her servile companions laughed and joked too, but they did not feel particularly mirthful; the household did not much like it, when their mistress was in a lively mood, for, to begin with, she expected from everyone prompt and complete participation in her merriment and was furious if anyone showed a face that did not beam with delight; and secondly, these outbursts never lasted long with her, and were usually followed by a sour and gloomy mood.

That day she had got up in a lucky hour; at cards she took the four knaves, which means the fulfilment of one's wishes (she used to try her fortune on the cards every morning), and her tea struck her as particularly delicious, for which her maid was rewarded by words of praise, and by two pence in money.

With a sweet smile on her wrinkled lips, the lady walked about the drawing-room and went up to the window. A flower-garden had been laid out before the window, and in the very middle bed, under a rosebush, lay Mumu busily gnawing a bone. The lady caught sight of her.

"Mercy on us!" she cried suddenly; "what dog is that?"

The companion, addressed by the old lady, hesitated, poor thing, in that wretched state of uneasiness which is common in any person in a dependent position who doesn't know very well what significance to give to the exclamation of a superior.

"I d... d... don't know," she faltered; "I fancy it's the dumb man's dog."

"Mercy!" the lady cut her short; "but it's a charming little dog! order it to be brought in. Has he had it long? How is it I've never seen it before?... Order it to be brought in."

The companion flew at once into the hall.

"Boy, boy!" she shouted; "bring Mumu in at once! She's in the flower-garden."

"Her name's Mumu then," observed the lady; "a very nice name."

"Oh, very, indeed!" chimed in the companion. "Make haste, Stepan!"

Stepan, a sturdy-built young fellow, whose duties were those of a footman, rushed headlong into the flower-garden, and tried to capture Mumu, but she cleverly slipped from his fingers, and with her tail in the air, fled full speed to Gerasim, who was at that instant in the kitchen, knocking out and cleaning a barrel, turning it upside down in his hands like a child's drum.
Stepan ran after her and tried to catch her just at her master's feet; but the sensible dog would not let a stranger touch her, and with a bound, she got away.

Gerasim looked on with a smile at all this ado; at last, Stepan got up, much amazed, and hurriedly explained to him by signs that the mistress wanted the dog brought in to her. Gerasim was a little astonished; he called Mumu, however, picked her up, and handed her over to Stepan.

Stepan carried her into the drawing-room and put her down on the parquet floor. The old lady began calling the dog to her in a coaxing voice. Mumu, who had never in her life been in such magnificent apartments, was very much frightened, and made a rush for the door, but, being driven back by the obsequious Stepan, she began trembling, and huddled close up against the wall.

"Mumu, Mumu, come to me, come to your mistress," said the lady; "come, silly thing... don't be afraid."

"Come, Mumu, come to the mistress," repeated the companions. "Come along!"

But Mumu looked around her uneasily and did not stir.

"Bring her something to eat," said the old lady. "How stupid she is! she won't come to her mistress. What's she afraid of?"

"She's not used to you yet," ventured one of the companions in a timid and conciliatory voice.

Stepan brought in a saucer of milk, and set it down before Mumu, but Mumu would not even sniff at the milk, and still shivered, and looked around as before.

"Ah, what a silly you are!" said the lady, and going up to her, she stooped down, and was about to stroke her, but Mumu turned her head abruptly, and showed her teeth. The lady hurriedly drew back her hand...

A momentary silence followed. Mumu gave a faint whine, as though she would complain and apologize... The old lady moved back, scowling. The dog's sudden movement had frightened her.

"Ah!" shrieked all the companions at once, "she's not bitten you, has she? Heaven forbidden! (Mumu had never bitten any one in her life.) Ah! ah!"

"Take her away," said the old lady in a changed voice. "Wretched little dog! What a spiteful creature!"

And, turning around deliberately, she went towards her boudoir. Her companions looked timidly at one another, and were about to follow her, but she stopped, stared coldly at them, and said, "What's that for, pray? I've not called you," and went out.

The companions waved their hands to Stepan in despair. He picked up Mumu, and flung her promptly outside the door, just at Gerasim's feet, and half an hour later a profound stillness led in the house, and the old lady sat on her sofa looking blacker than a thundercloud.

What trifles, if you think of it, will sometimes disturb any one!

Till evening the lady was out of humor; she did not talk to anyone, did not play cards, and passed a bad night.

She fancied the eau-de-Cologne they gave her was not the same as she usually had, and that her pillow smelt of soap, and she made the wardrobe-maid smell all the bed linen in fact she was very upset and cross altogether.

Next morning, she ordered Gavrila to be summoned an hour earlier than usual.

"Tell me, please," she began, directly the latter, not without some inward trepidation, crossed the threshold of her boudoir, "what dog was that barking all night in our yard? It wouldn't let me sleep!"

"A dog, 'm... what dog, 'm... may be, the dumb man's dog, 'm," he brought out in a rather unsteady voice.

"I don't know whether it was the dumb man's or whose, but it wouldn't let me sleep. And I wonder what we have such a lot of dogs for! I wish to know. We have a yard dog, haven't we?"

"Oh yes, 'm, we have, 'm. Wolf, 'm."

"Well, why more? What do we want more dogs for? It's simply introducing disorder. There's no one in control in the house—that's what it is. And what does the dumb man want with a dog? Who gave him leave to keep dogs in my yard? Yesterday I went to the window, and there it was lying in the flower-garden; it had dragged in nastiness it was gnawing, and my roses are planted there..."

The lady ceased.

"Let her be gone from to-day... do you hear?"

"Yes, 'm."

"To-day. Now go. I will send for you later for the report."

Gavrila went away. As he went through the drawing-room, the steward, by way of maintaining order, moved a bell from one table to another; he stealthily blew his duck-like nose in the hall, and went into the outer-hall.

In the outer-hall, on a locker, was Stepan asleep in the attitude of a slain warrior in a battalion picture, his bare legs thrust out below the coat which served him for a blanket.

The steward gave him a shove, and whispered some instructions to him, to which Stepan responded with something between a yawn and a laugh. The steward went away, and Stepan got up, put on his coat and his boots, went out and stood on the steps.

Five minutes had not passed before Gerasim made his appearance with a huge bundle of hewn logs on his back, accompanied by the inseparable Mumu. (The lady had given orders that her bedroom and boudoir should be heated at times even in the summer.)

Gerasim turned sideways before the door, shoved it open with his shoulder, and staggered into the house with his load. Mumu, as usual, stayed behind to wait for him.

Then Stepan, seizing his chance, suddenly pounced on her, like a kite on a chicken, held her down to the ground, gathered her up in his arms, and without even putting on his cap, ran out of the yard with her, got into the first fly he met, and galloped off to a market-place.

There he soon found a purchaser, to whom he sold her for a shilling, on condition that he would keep her for at least a week tied up; then he returned at once. But before he got home, he got off the fly, and going right around the yard, jumped over the fence into the yard from a back street. He was afraid to go in at the gate for fear of meeting Gerasim.

He is anxiety was unnecessary, however; Gerasim was no longer in the yard. On coming out of the house he had at once missed Mumu. He never remembered her failing to wait for his return, and began running up and down, looking for her, and calling her in his own way...

He rushed up to his garret, up to the hay-loft, ran out into the street, this way and that...

She was lost! He turned to the other serfs, with the most despairing signs, questioned them about her, pointing to her height from the ground, describing her with his hands... Some of them really did not know what had become of Mumu, and merely shook their heads; others did know, and smiled to him for all response; while the steward assumed an important air and began scolding the busmen.

Then Gerasim ran right away out of the yard. It was dark by the time he came back. From his worn-out look, his unsteady walk, and his dusty clothes, it might be surmised that he had been running over half Moscow.

He stood still opposite the windows of the mistress's house, took a searching look at the steps where a group of house-serfs were crowded together, turned away, and uttered once more his inarticulate "Mumu."

Mumu did not answer. He went away. Everyone looked after him, but no one smiled or said a word, and the inquisitive postilion.

Antipka reported next morning in the kitchen that the dumb man had been groaning all night.

All the next day Gerasim did not show himself, so that they were obliged to send the busman Potap for water instead of him, at which the busman Potap was anything but pleased.

The lady asked Gavrila if her orders had been carried out. Gavrila replied that they had.

The next morning Gerasim came out of his garret and went about his work. He came in to his dinner, ate it, and went out again, without a greeting to anyone. His face, which had always been lifeless, as with all deaf-mutes, seemed now to be turned to stone. After dinner he went out of the yard again, but not for long; he came back, and went straight up to the hayloft.

Night came on, a clear moonlight night. Gerasim lay breathing heavily, and incessantly turning from side to side.

Suddenly he felt something pull at the skirt of his coat. He started, but did not raise his head, and even shut his eyes tighter.

But again, there was a pull, stronger than before; he jumped up before him, with an end of string around her neck, was Mumu, twisting and turning.

A prolonged cry of delight broke from his speechless breast; he caught up Mumu, and hugged her tight in his arms, she licked his nose and eyes, and beard and moustache, all in one instant...

He stood a little, thought a minute, crept cautiously down from the hay-loft, looked around, and having satisfied himself that no one could see him, made his way successfully to his garret.

Gerasim had guessed before that his dog had not got lost by her own doing, that she must have been taken away by the mistress's orders; the servants had explained to him by signs that his Mumu had snapped at her, and he determined to take his own measures.

First, he fed Mumu with a bit of bread, fondled her, and put her to bed, then he fell to meditating, and spent the whole night long in meditating how he could best conceal her. At last he decided to leave her all day in the garret, and only to come in now and then to see her, and to take her out at night.

The hole in the door he stopped up effectually with his old overcoat, and almost before it was light he was already in the yard, as though nothing had happened, even—innocent-guile! the same expression of melancholy on his face.

It did not even occur to the poor deaf man that Mumu would betray herself by her whining; in reality, everyone in the house was soon aware that the dumb man's dog had come back, and was locked up in his garret, but from sympathy with him and with her, and partly, perhaps, from dread of him, they did not let him know that they had found out his secret.

The steward scratched his head, and gave a despairing wave of his head, as much as to say, "Well, well, God have mercy on him! If only it doesn't come to the mistress's ears!"

But the dumb man had never shown such energy as on that day; he cleaned and scraped the whole courtyard, pulled up every single weed with his own hand, tugged up every stake in the fence of the flower-garden, to satisfy himself that they were strong enough, and unaided drove them in again; in fact, he toiled and labored so that even the old lady noticed his zeal.

Twice in the course of the day Gerasim went stealthily in to see his prisoner; when night came on, he lay down to sleep with her in the garret, not in the hay-loft, and only at two o'clock in the night he went out to take her a turn in the fresh air.

After walking about the courtyard, a good while with her, he was just turning back, when suddenly a rustle was heard behind the fence on the side of the back street.

Mumu pricked up her ears, growled—went up to the fence, sniffed, and gave vent to a loud shrill bark. Some drunkard had thought fit to take refuge under the fence for the night. At that very time the old lady had just fallen asleep after a prolonged fit of "nervous agitation"; these fits of agitation always overtook her after too hearty a supper.
The sudden bark waked her up: her heart palpitated, and she felt faint.

"Girls, girls!" she moaned. "Girls!" The terrified maids ran into her bedroom. "Oh, oh, I am dying!" she said, flinging her arms about in her agitation. "Again, that dog, again!... Oh, send for the doctor. They mean to be the death of me... The dog, the dog again! Oh!"

And she let her head fall back, which always signified a swoon. They rushed for the doctor, that is, for the household physician, Hariton. This doctor, whose whole qualification consisted in wearing soft-soled boots, knew how to feel the pulse delicately.

He used to sleep fourteen hours out of the twenty-four, but the rest of the time he was always sighing, and continually dosing the old lady with cherry bay drops.

This doctor ran up at once, fumigated the room with burnt feathers, and when the old lady opened her eyes, promptly offered her a wineglass of the hallowed drops on a silver tray.

The old lady took them but began again at once in a tearful voice complaining of the dog, of Gavrila, and of her fate, declaring that she was a poor old woman, and that everyone had forsaken her, no one pitied her, everyone wished her dead. Meanwhile the luckless Mumu had gone on barking, while Gerasim tried in vain to call her away, from the fence. "There... there... again," groaned the old lady, and once more she turned up the whites of her eyes.

The doctor whispered to a maid, she rushed into the outer hall, and shook Stepan, he ran to wake Gavrila, Gavrila in a fury ordered the whole household to get up.

Gerasim turned around, saw lights and shadows moving in the windows, and with an instinct of coming trouble in his heart, put Mumu under his arm, ran into his garret, and locked himself in.

A few minutes later five men were banging at his door, but feeling the resistance of the bolt, they stopped. Gavrila ran up in a fearful state of mind and ordered them all to wait there and watch till morning.

Then he flew off himself to the maids' quarter, and through an old companion, Liubov Liubimovna, with whose assistance he used to steal tea, sugar, and other groceries and to falsify the accounts, sent word to the mistress that the dog had unhappily run back from somewhere, but that to-morrow she should be killed, and would the mistress be so gracious as not to be angry and to overlook it. The old lady would probably not have been so soon appeased, but the doctor had in his haste given her fully forty drops instead of twelve.

The strong dose of narcotic acted; in a quarter of an hour the old lady was in a sound and peaceful sleep; while Gerasim was lying with a white face on his bed, holding Mumu's mouth tightly shut.

Next morning the lady woke up rather late. Gavrila was waiting till she should be awake, to give the order for a final assault on Gerasim's stronghold, while he prepared himself to face a fearful storm. But the storm did not come off. The old lady lay in bed and sent for the eldest of her dependent companions.

"Liubov Liubimovna," she began in a subdued weak voice— she was fond of playing the part of an oppressed and forsaken victim; needless to say, everyone in the house was made extremely uncomfortable at such times—

"Liubov Liubimovna, you see my position; go, my love, to Gavrila Andreitch, and talk to him a little. Can he really prize some wretched cur above the repose—the very life—of his mistress? I could not bear to think so," she added, with an expression of deep feeling. "Go, my love; be so good as to go to Gavrila Andreitch for me."

Liubov Liubimovna went to Gavrila's room. What conversation passed between them is not known, but a short time after, a whole crowd of people was moving across the yard in the direction of Gerasim's garret. Gavrila walked in front, holding his cap on with his hand, though there was no wind.

The footmen and cooks were close behind him; Uncle Tail was looking out of a window, giving instructions, that is to say, simply waving his hands. At the rear there was a crowd of small boys skipping and hopping along; half of them were outsiders who had run up.

On the narrow staircase leading to the garret sat one guard; at the door were standing two more with sticks. They began to mount the stairs, which they entirely blocked up. Gavrila went up to the door, knocked with his fist, shouting, "Open the door!" A stifled bark was audible, but there was no answer.

"Open the door, I tell you," he repeated.

"But, Gavrila Andreitch," Stepan observed from below, "he's deaf, you know—he doesn't hear."

They all laughed.

"What are we to do?" Gavrila rejoined from above.

"Why, there's a hole there in the door," answered Stepan, "so you shake the stick in there."

Gavrila bent down.

"He's stuffed it up with a coat or something."

"Well, you just push the coat in."

At this moment a smothered bark was heard again.

"See, see—she speaks for herself," was remarked in the crowd, and again they laughed.

Gavrila scratched his ear.

"No, mate," he responded at last, "you can poke the coat in yourself, if you like."

"All right, let me."

And Stepan scrambled up, took the stick, pushed in the coat, and began waving the stick about in the opening, saying, "Come out, come out!" as he did so. He was still waving the stick, when suddenly the door of the garret was flung open; all the crowd flew pell-mell down the stairs instantly, Gavrila first of all. Uncle Tail locked the window.

"Come, come, come," shouted Gavrila from the yard, "mind what you're about."

Gerasim stood without stirring in his doorway. The crowd gathered at the foot of the stairs. Gerasim, with his arms akimbo, looked down at all these poor creatures in German coats; in his red peasant's shirt he looked like a giant before them. Gavrila took a step forward.

"Mind, mate," said he, "don't be insolent."

And he began to explain to him by signs that the mistress insists on having his dog; that he must hand it over at once, or it would be the worse for him.

Gerasim looked at him, pointed to the dog, made a motion with his hand around his neck, as though he were pulling a noose tight, and glanced with a face of inquiry at the steward.

"Yes, yes," the latter assented, nodding; "yes, just so."

Gerasim dropped his eyes, then all of a sudden roused himself and pointed to Mumu, who was all the while standing beside him, innocently wagging her tail and pricking up her ears inquisitively. Then he repeated the strangling action around his neck and significantly struck himself on the breast, as though announcing he would take upon himself the task of killing Mumu.

"But you'll deceive us," Gavrila waved back in response.

Gerasim looked at him, smiled scornfully, struck himself again on the breast, and slammed to the door.

They all looked at one another in silence.

"What does that mean?" Gavrila began. "He's locked himself in."

"Let him be, Gavrila Andreitch," Stepan advised; "he'll do it if he's promised. He's like that, you know... If he makes a promise, it's a certain thing. He's not like us others in that. The truth's the truth with him. Yes, indeed."

"Yes," they all repeated, nodding their heads, "yes—that's so—yes."

Uncle Tail opened his window, and he too said, "Yes."

"Well, may be, we shall see," responded Gavrila; "any way, we won't take off the guard. Here you, Eroshka!" he added, addressing a poor fellow in a yellow nankeen coat, who considered himself to be a gardener, "what have you to do? Take a stick and sit here, and if anything happens, run to me at once!"

Eroshka took a stick and sat down on the bottom stair.

The crowd dispersed, all except a few inquisitive small boys, while Gavrila went home and sent word through Liubov Liubimovna to the mistress that everything had been done, while he sent a postilion for a policeman in case of need. The old lady tied a knot in her handkerchief, sprinkled some eau-de-Cologne on it, sniffed at it, and rubbed her temples with it, drank some tea, and, being still under the influence of the cherry bay drops, fell asleep again.

An hour after all this hubbub the garret door opened, and Gerasim showed himself. He had on his best coat; he was leading Mumu by a string. Eroshka moved aside and let him pass.

Gerasim went to the gates. All the small boys in the yard stared at him in silence. He did not even turn around; he only put his cap on in the street. Gavrila sent the same Eroshka to follow him and keep watch on him as a spy.

Eroshka, seeing from a distance that he had gone into a cookshop with his dog, waited for him to come out again.

Gerasim was well known at the cookshop, and his signs were understood. He asked for cabbage soup with meat in it and sat down with his arms on the table. Mumu stood beside his chair, looking calmly at him with her intelligent eyes. Her coat was glossy; one could see she had just been combed down.

They brought Gerasim the soup. He crumbled some bread into it, cut the meat up small, and put the plate on the ground. Mumu began eating in her usual refined way, her little muzzle daintily held so as scarcely to touch her food.

Gerasim gazed a long while at her; two big tears suddenly rolled from his eyes; one fell on the dog's brow, the other into the soup. He shaded his face with his hand. Mumu ate up half the plateful, and came away from it, licking her lips. Gerasim got up, paid for the soup, and went out, followed by the rather perplexed glances of the waiter.

Eroshka, seeing Gerasim, hid around a corner, and letting him get in front, followed him again.

Gerasim walked without haste, still holding Mumu by a string. When he got to the corner of the street, he stood still as though reflecting, and suddenly set off with rapid steps to the Crimean Ford.

On the way he went into the yard of a house, where a lodge was being built, and carried away two bricks under his arm. At the Crimean Ford, he turned along the bank, went to a place where there were two little rowing-boats fastened to stakes (he had noticed them there before), and jumped into one of them with Mumu.

A lame old man came out of a shed in the corner of a kitchen-garden and shouted after him; but Gerasim only nodded, and began rowing so vigorously, though against stream, that in an instant he had darted two hundred yards way.

The old man stood for a while, scratched his back first with the left and then with the right hand, and went back hobbling to the shed.

Gerasim rowed on and on. Moscow was soon left behind. Meadows stretched each side of the bank, market gardens, fields, and copses; peasants' huts began to make their appearance.

There was the fragrance of the country. He threw down his oars, bent his head down to Mumu, who was sitting facing him on a dry cross seat—the bottom of the boat was full of water—and stayed motionless, his mighty hands clasped upon her back, while the boat was gradually carried back by the current towards the town.

At last Gerasim drew himself up hurriedly, with a sort of sick anger in his face, he tied up the bricks he had taken with string, made a running noose, put it around Mumu's neck, lifted her up over the river, and for the last time looked at her...

She watched him confidingly and without any fear, faintly wagging her tail. He turned away, frowned, and wrung his hands...

Gerasim heard nothing, neither the quick shrill whine of Mumu as she fell, nor the heavy splash of the water; for him the noisiest day was soundless and silent as even the stillest night is not silent to us.

When he opened his eyes again, little wavelets were hurrying over the river, chasing one another; as before they broke against the boat's side, and only far away behind wide circles moved widening to the bank.

Directly Gerasim had vanished from Eroshka's sight, the latter returned home and reported what he had seen.

"Well, then," observed Stepan, "he'll drown her. Now we can feel easy about it. If he once promises a thing..."

No one saw Gerasim during the day. He did not have dinner at home. Evening came on; they were all gathered together to supper, except him.

"What a strange creature that Gerasim is!" piped a fat laundrymaid; "fancy, upsetting himself like that over a dog... Upon my word!"

"But Gerasim has been here," Stepan cried all at once, scraping up his porridge with a spoon.

"How? when?"

"Why, a couple of hours ago. Yes, indeed! I ran against him at the gate; he was going out again from here; he was coming out of the yard. I tried to ask him about his dog, but he wasn't in the best of humors, I could see. Well, he gave me a shove; I suppose he only meant to put me out of his way, as if he'd say, 'Let me go, do!' but he fetched me such a crack on my neck, so seriously, that—oh! oh!"

And Stepan, who could not help laughing, shrugged up and rubbed the back of his head. "Yes," he added; "he has got a fist; it's something like a fist, there's no denying that!"

They all laughed at Stepan, and after supper they separated to go to bed.

Meanwhile, at that very time, a gigantic figure with a bag on his shoulders and a stick in his hand, was eagerly and persistently stepping out along the T—- high-road.

It was Gerasim. He was hurrying on without looking around; hurrying homewards, to his own village, to his own country.

After drowning poor Mumu, he had run back to his garret, hurriedly packed a few things together in an old horsecloth, tied it up in a bundle, tossed it on his shoulder, and so was ready.

He had noticed the road carefully when he was brought to Moscow; the village his mistress had taken him from lay only about twenty miles off the high-road.

He walked along it with a sort of invincible purpose, a desperate and at the same time joyous determination. He walked, his shoulders thrown back and his chest expanded; his eyes were fixed greedily straight before him.

He hastened as though his old mother were waiting for him at home, as though she were calling him to her after long wanderings in strange parts, among strangers.

92

The summer night, that was just drawing in, was still and warm; on one side, where the sun had set, the horizon was still light and faintly flushed with the last glow of the vanished day; on the other side a blue-gray twilight had already risen up. The night was coming up from that quarter. Quails were in hundreds around; corncrakes were calling to one another in the thickets...

Gerasim could not hear them; he could not hear the delicate night-whispering of the trees, by which his strong legs carried him, but he smelt the familiar scent of the ripening rye, which was wafted from the dark fields; he felt the wind, flying to meet him—the wind from home—beat caressingly upon his face, and play with his hair and his beard. He saw before him the whitening road homewards, straight as an arrow.

He saw in the sky stars innumerable, lighting up his way, and stepped out, strong and bold as a lion, so that when the rising sun shed its moist rosy light upon the still fresh and unwearied traveller, already thirty miles lay between him and Moscow.

In a couple of days, he was at home, in his little hut, to the great astonishment of the soldier's wife who had been put in there. After praying before the holy pictures, he set off at once to the village elder.

The village elder was at first surprised; but the hay-cutting had just begun; Gerasim was a first-rate mower, and they put a scythe into his hand on the spot, and he went to mow in his old way, mowing so that the peasants were fairly astounded as they watched his wide sweeping strokes and the heaps he raked together...

In Moscow the day after Gerasim's flight they missed him. They went to his garret, rummaged about in it, and spoke to Gavrila. He came, looked, shrugged his shoulders, and decided that the dumb man had either run away or had drowned himself with his stupid dog.

They gave information to the police and informed the lady. The old lady was furious, burst into tears, gave orders that he was to be found whatever happened, declared she had never ordered the dog to be destroyed, and, in fact, gave Gavrila such a rating that he could do nothing all day but shake his head and murmur, "Well!" until Uncle Tail checked him at last, sympathetically echoing "We-ell!"

At last the news came from the country of Gerasim's being there. The old lady was somewhat pacified; at first, she issued a mandate for him to be brought back without delay to Moscow; afterwards, however, she declared that such an ungrateful creature was absolutely of no use to her. Soon after this she died herself; and her heirs had no thought to spare for Gerasim; they let their mother's other servants redeem their freedom on payment of an annual rent.

And Gerasim is living still, a lonely man in his lonely hut; he is strong and healthy as before, and does the work of four men as before, and as before is serious and steady.

But his neighbours have observed that ever since his return from Moscow he has quite given up the society of women; he will not even look at them and does not keep even a single dog.

"It's his good luck, though," the peasants reason, "that he can get on without female folk; and as for a dog—what need has he of a dog? you wouldn't get a thief to go into his yard for any money!" Such is the fame of the dumb man's Titanic strength.

11. Christmas Impression of a Deaf Boy

Hurray, vacation! We're going home! Hendrik thought
enthusiastically after waking up one December morning in the
dormitory of the Institute for Deaf children in the north of the
Netherlands. A little later, after washing and getting dressed, he
noticed that all the boys, even the most sluggish, were already
ready. No wonder: they were so excited by the thought of going
home today.

Hendrik quickly hopped down the stairs into the dining
room. After breakfast they waited until it was time to leave. Near
the wall behind the billiard table, the large, thick brown suitcases
were also "waiting." Finally, it was time and one by one the boys
left to go home with a parent. A large group left all at once,
accompanied by a teacher, who walked to the station with the boys
and the girls. One of the boys went all the way to Limburg by train,
where his parents lived. The others went to The Hague,
unimaginably far away for Hendrik. He felt the fingers of Hiltje, his
deaf elder sister, tapping his arm rather hard and noticed her happy
face. Hendrik laughed and asked her if their father was already
there. She nodded her head a few times in answer. The father stood
laughing, looking at them from the door.

Within half an hour they were at the bus station. The bus was
ready to leave and the three of them boarded. Sitting on a leather
chair in the bus, Hendrik felt more confident. Homewards! In the
large village, forty-five kilometers away, Hendrik, his father, and
his sister got out. Tasma, the friendly garage owner, was already
there with his car. They needed to travel by car because it was too
cold to walk. Hendrik enjoyed it even though it only lasted ten
minutes. The passengers got out of the car on the paved road.

Hendrik saw his mother and his beloved dog, called Mora, standing there, and he ran to them on the sand path. When it rained a lot, the path could quickly change into a row of mud puddles. Fortunately, it was perfectly passable today.

More than one week later, it was different. On Christmas Day, everything was covered by the long-awaited snow. After the hasty lunch (father was busy milking the cows) the whole family stepped out into the evening air.

Oh, oh, how cold it was. In the countryside it's often dark as soon as you step outside the door. That's why Hendrik saw bright stars shining everywhere. On the paved road, Hendrik looked up every now and then. His ears hurt; it seemed as if the sharp cold bit into his ears. He saw some people coming from their farms. They too went to the Sunday school, Hendrik knew. Oh, how beautiful those stars in the sky were. Hendrik was reminded of the Christmas story in the book at the school for the deaf children. That coloring plate showed lots of stars, angels, and shepherds. So beautiful. Now again, Hendrik saw with his own eyes the many stars sparkling against the dark sky.

That is where God lives. But there are now no angels or shepherds. Hendrik continued to dream about the birth of the Lord Jesus.

The large procession of people and children stopped at the church building. Hendrik shuddered for a moment as he sat between his parents on the bench, among the many other people in the warm church. Hendrik was very jealous of his oldest sister, because she was sitting in front with her hearing friends. During the evening, Hendrik shuffled back and forth on the bench. He could hardly see what was happening at the altar, because there was a broad-shouldered adult sitting in front of him.

Hendrik did see a glimpse of a very large and beautifully decorated Christmas tree, and the leader of the Sunday school. That man sang and his mouth moved, and Hendrik looked at it with fascination. Moments later, he saw two large girls walking around with a white can full of hot chocolate. Hendrik very much looked forward to having some. But his mother gave him a peppermint, which he didn't care for particularly. He much preferred hot chocolate. He saw his little sister at the exit of the church holding a booklet and an orange. He looked at it with covetous eyes. At home, his father told him that next year he would be old enough to be allowed to sit at the front of the church too.

12. Bad Luck Journey

Several weeks ago, Koen Terwegt had come into possession of a second-hand car, an NSU-Prinz. Having obtained his driver's license after much trouble, he was now overjoyed with his car. But he wasn't sure about driving it. Suppose something would go wrong with the car? He had no technical skills and he didn't have the money to visit a garage for every single issue. His friends underlined the importance of knowing something about the inner workings of his car.

So, it was no wonder that Koen jumped for joy when he read about a course about "Breakdown on the road" by the AAA in a national magazine for deaf people. That was his kind of thing, Koen decided. But as he read on, he let out a sigh of disappointment. It was way too far away from him—in Rotterdam—while he lived in Oosterbeek. Yet for the rest of the day, the idea of the course stayed in his mind.

"I want to go and so I will go," he thought bitterly.

Because he was not entirely sure of his driving skills, he took the train and he arrived on a Friday evening at the Central Station in Rotterdam. From there he walked while looking through the quarter of the city, but he did not find the location of the AAA station. That was, until he suddenly saw a number of people walking, who were using sign language. Contact was quickly made and yes, they could tell him where he needed to go. It was not far anymore. The course, however, was a bitter disappointment for Koen, because it was difficult to follow the spoken instructions; also, he was absolutely not technically skilled. The instructor sometimes talked too quickly and there was no interpreter for deaf people at that time. After the course, which only lasted one night, Koen returned to the train station with a dissatisfied feeling. It was all too theoretical; even though he had received a folder with information from the instructor, in his opinion it was by no means sufficient.

He stood alone on the platform and waited for the half-past-ten train. Every now and then he looked at the station clock.

Strange, it was already a minute late and there was still no train. He knew for sure that he was on the right platform. Suddenly he saw how a few platforms further on, a train slowly drove off.

Something is wrong here, Koen thought worriedly.

A man wearing a dark red cap that indicated he worked for the railways, walked in his direction and Koen asked him where his train was. The conversation that followed took a lot of time. The communication did not run too smoothly; the man talked under his breath. At last Koen understood that it had been announced that his train to Arnhem was departing from another platform and was already driving off. The railway man lifted his heels and left an angry, outraged Koen behind. He could only stamp the ground impotently. There was nothing else but to make the best of it; so, he quickly walked to a big sign with travel information.

Behind a blurred pane, the late traveler studied the departure times with some difficulty, but he had to establish that he could not go any further that night than to Utrecht.

Well, all right then, he thought bravely.

After ten minutes of waiting, Koen left arrived in Utrecht at a quarter to twelve and found a hotel opposite the station. Hesitantly, he stepped into the large night quarters. The man at the front desk told him that the hotel was full. All of a sudden it crossed his mind that he could check whether there might be a bus to go home. Determined, Koen stepped back into the cold evening air. At the bus station he looked around for a bus in the right direction.

Hah, he thought pleased, *here is one*.

He quickly discovered the neon-lit word "Woudenberg" on the front of the bus and then checked the departure time. That was not too bad. It was about to leave. When Koen arrived in Woudenberg, he was the only passenger and he could not go any further that night; there was no other bus. He walked idly through the sleeping village and looked at the illuminated hands of his watch: ten to one. Luckily, he knew the area pretty well and he decided to try and find the motorway. His plan was to hitchhike. Soon he found a brightly lit traffic sign; he was on the right track. He walked on.

What an adventure and in February too! It drizzled and the wind began to pick up, but nevertheless Koen posted himself on the side of the motorway.

He couldn't count the number of times he put his thumb up for a ride. It was getting colder and, occasionally, Koen shivered violently, but apparently nobody was going to give him a ride. But walking any further made no sense either; it was much too far to Oosterbeek. I'll keep trying to hitchhike, he thought. The headlights of the cars waved past him. No one considered giving him a ride and he was angry with the cold-hearted drivers. To his surprise, hardly any trucks drove by. Finally, at half past five, a big American car stopped just in front of him.

At last, he thought happily, although at the same time he was startled by the long-haired occupants.

He managed to make the young people understand him and he got into the big car. Within 45 minutes, they dropped Koen off at the intersection near his landlady's house.

He stammered, "Thank you" and got out, his arms waving wildly.

It had been an evening full of bad luck. After some years he found out, to his surprise, that hitchhiking on the motorway was not allowed. He had never really known that.

13.   A Deaf Prisoner

My mustache is not good at all! Jan Hake sighs deeply when he sees himself in the bathroom mirror. *I look a lot like a terrorist.* His friends have also told him that. His face just does not look so friendly with the mustache.

Shall I shave it off? he asks himself.

He has had the mustache for half a year. He takes a pair of scissors, hesitates…

"No, I'll do it when the carnival is over," Jan gestures toward his reflection in the mirror.

Then he looks at his watch and is shocked. It is already time to leave. It is high time to go to his training. On the street on his bike, Jan is astonished to see many police cars with their blue flashing lights. Suddenly, he feels his arm being grabbed from behind.

He has to stop cycling and hits the top tube of his bicycle. Oh, that hurts a lot!

He thinks, *this is too crazy. What is happening to me? All these officers are surrounding me.*

He has to drop his bike on the ground because they quickly handcuff him. He wants to resist, but still clearly feels something pressed into his back. Afraid, he walks in between a few officers to a car. Suddenly Jan realizes something. But, of course: the day before yesterday he happened to read something in the newspaper about a terrorist act in the city. He hardly ever reads the newspaper, there are far too many difficult words.

Jan thinks, *the police must think I am a nice catch. What now?*

He looks at the policeman next to him and is about to ask what it is all about. But that man looks straight ahead. Desperately, he wonders whether he has an identity card on him, his driving license or something. His right hand is going up to the inside pocket of his jacket, but immediately he gets a punch.

"Ouch," he grunts.

What a stupid thing not to cut off my mustache...Pure vanity. Too bad, now I'm really in trouble. Oh well. I'll explain to the police that they are mistaken. I can talk. Yes. I learned that at the deaf school; talking and having a voice.

Unfortunately for Jan no one understands him at the police station. Maybe the problem is also that he does not look very Dutch. They just think he is a foreigner who speaks Dutch very badly. A man in civilian clothes comes into the room, but he talks too fast. His piercing eyes make Jan uncomfortable and he laughs nervously.

Too crazy! So many people surrounding me, so much interest in me.

Van Haasteren sees him laughing and suddenly becomes angry. He makes an unexpected move with his arm, which makes Jan almost fall off his chair.

Then he is taken to a cell by two burly policemen. Sitting on the wooden bench, Jan checks his watch; it's 9 o'clock. Outside it is already dark. A long night awaits him.

Annoying. No one can understand me. How is it possible? Yes, the prisoner nods to himself. *The deaf school was worthless. There, he was not allowed to make gestures with his peers. Why not?*

He suddenly realizes how strange it all is. Why can *hearing* people understand each other so easily? And why can deaf people understand each other so well? He shakes his head. His parents, yes, they understand him much better. Despite the pressing advice of the director of the deaf school, they used hand gestures, especially for him. That was really nice. Jan smiles at that. But then his face tightens. Too bad, his parents won't come back from their holiday until tomorrow…

He starts to bang with his fists on the door of his cell but nothing happens, and he has to stop, because he cannot stand the pain for very long. He is angry at those stupid policemen who only shrug their shoulders. Then Jan realizes how stupid he himself is. Recently, he received a card with "I AM DEAF" printed on it in blue letters He threw away the beautifully designed card.

And now this, Jan thinks sadly.

He stays awake for a long time. He thinks long about the disadvantages of being deaf. Hearing people don't understand anything. His colleagues at the factory do not either. It's hopeless…

Suddenly he gets a good idea. Yes, he should try tomorrow with the hand alphabet that he learned from his deaf friends at the other deaf school. And finally, he falls asleep.

The following morning, Jan is already awake when someone comes to his cell. And yes, the door opens.

The prisoner's fingers begin to move slowly, "I am innocent, I am not a criminal."

The man who opened the door looks with strained attention at Jan's moving fingers. That gives him courage and he continues to use his fingers. It's the ideal communication tool he has learned from his friends at another school for deaf children who use the sign language and the hand alphabet. It really seems to work, because a man beckons him to follow him. He is offered coffee and bread and in the course of the morning he sees a familiar face: the sign language interpreter enters the room with the other police chief. Finally, he is released.

When he gets home, he first goes to the bathroom. Without hesitation he grabs the scissors and cuts off most of his mustache and then uses the shaver to remove the rest. Jan grins at himself in the mirror. By the evening, his parents are back and, of course, Jan tells them of his "adventure" at the police station.

14.   The eternal struggle[3]

It is for the parents never easy to be confronted with the deafness of their child. Of course, they count on a normal health of their baby. So, when an audiologist after a hearing test with a baby draws the conclusion that the child is deaf, that is often dramatic. The parents may actually resist the diagnoses, it's a natural response. Such parents should immediately be assisted. Other parents who have gone through similar issues can be of great assistance and there are also professionals who specialize in these cases. In the following excerpt, the authors describe how a couple of such parents after a few years received a second blow of another nature.

Chapter 16

"Baby-sitter's here", I called to Louise. Bruce ran through the living room to answer the doorbell. It was shortly after seven o'clock and the gray darkness of an early November evening had already settled over Sacramento. The parents' meeting at Starr King Exceptional School would start in twenty minutes.

"I hope you don't have too much trouble with Lynn tonight", Louise said to Pat Kerns who was talking off her coat.

"We won't be late; it's a meeting at the school. She should go to bed about nine o'clock, and if you have trouble, Bruce can probably make her understand." Reluctant to leave Lynn with

[3] *Reprinted by permission of the publisher from Deaf Like me by Thomas S. Spradley and James P. Spradley (Washington DC: Gallaudet Press 1985: 200-226). Copyright @ 1978 by Thomas S. Spradley and James P. Spradley*

someone she did not know, someone with whom she could not communicate, we felt lucky to have found sixteen-year old Pat. She only lived a few houses down the street.

"She's good with kids", her mother, Lois Kerns, had told Louise a few weeks after we moved into the neighborhood.

"And she can always call me if there is a problem."

"Hi! Glad you both could come tonight." Fred Hockett, the principal of Starr King, stood near one of the doors to a large room that during the day had a partition down the middle to form two pre-school classrooms.
A gold tweed carpet gave warmth to the room.

We sat down beside Mrs. Conklin, Lynn's teacher, and waited while several more people came in. Nearly all of the more than twenty parents were still strangers to us.

We had moved to Sacramento as much for Starr King School as for my job at American River College. For Bruce, it hardly mattered where we moved. He could always count on a school and friends, but Lynn's future demanded careful planning and investigation.

Whenever I had heard of a possible teaching position, I immediately wrote to inquire about local programs for educating deaf children.

Was the school committed to an oral approach? Did special classes for the deaf end at age six or eight. What could we expect when Lynn reached high school age? Did the school system place deaf students in classes along with hearing? At some later date, we did not want to have to choose between sending Lynn away to a residential school or making still another move.

My letter to Starr King school had brought good news from Mr. Hockett.

"I feel our program is equal to any in the nation", he wrote. The school served one hundred children with speech and hearing disabilities. Their teachers had been trained at the John Tracy Clinic, Gallaudet College and the Clarke School for the Deaf. In high school, deaf children were integrated with the hearing. Most important, everyone at the school was deeply committed to using *only* the oral approach.

"I'd like to welcome you all", Dr. Mason, the school psychologist, said.

"Tonight, we thought it would be helpful to talk about discipline problems that you have with your deaf child. But before we break into small discussion groups, Barbara Simmons has an announcement that she wants to make."

He nodded in her direction and sat down. An attractive woman in her early thirties with a resolute manner rose to her feet in the second row on the left-hand side.

"A group of concerned parents from our school and some deaf people from the community are going to meet tomorrow night", said she.
"We will be discussing total communication and talking about using sign language along with speech and lip reading. Some of us have become interested in ways to improve communication with our deaf children. You are all welcome to join us. We will meet at the Sutter Hospital auditorium on F Street at seven-thirty."

A strange stillness hung in the air. No one spoke. I could feel the tension grow as the implications of this brief announcement ran through the minds of everyone present. Dr. Mason started to rise, hesitated, then got up to let us know how to organize our discussions.

"Not more than six to a group", he said quickly, avoiding any comment about Mrs. Simmons' announcement.

"And one teacher to each group. We'll spend about thirty minutes in small groups, then get back together to compare notes."

Before we stood up, Mrs. Conklin leaned over to Louise and spoke in a low voice.

"You both support the oralist philosophy, don't you?" When Louise nodded he continued.

"Our school is an *oral* school and we want it to remain *oral*. I'd stay away from that group of parents who want to use a manual approach."

It seemed strange to us that these parents were interested in sign language. Why would they want to start that kind of thing with four- or five-year-old? I thought to myself. Maybe their kids have other problems; maybe they just can't learn to lip-read and talk. I recalled the little girl in Lynn's class in Covina who could only understand a few words. We had heard of older children who failed to develop speech even here at Starr King.

At the insistence of the only teacher on the staff who knew sign language, a total communication class had been started at a nearby school for six twelve-year-old who couldn't talk or lip-read well enough to communicate. But failure to speak at age twelve couldn't be compared with an inability to speak at age five.

Louise and I moved our chairs over to one side of the room where several people had pushed their chairs up to small oval table. Mrs. Garvin, a preschool teacher, Barbara Simmons and several other parents joined us a d we all introduced ourselves.

Mrs. Garvin started the discussion with a question.

"Is anyone having discipline problems at home?"

I looked at the floor. A minute of silence finally ended when a woman across from Louise spoke.

"It's hard to get my boy to obey—like going to bed. He's stubborn, but mostly he just doesn't seem to understand. I never had problems like these with my two hearing children."

After a short pause Mrs. Garvin said, "You know, I think we sometimes treat deaf children different because we *feel* they're

108

different. We should treat them just like normal children. Expect them to obey. Insist that they obey.

Your child doesn't have to know what you say to follow a simple command like 'go to bed.''

"We have the same trouble with our daughter", I put in.

"We try to act the way we did with our son; I suppose sometimes we feel Lynn just doesn't understand, so we give her benefit of the doubt. We try to explain, but if she keeps refusing, we just have to resort to force."

"Is this a common problem with the rest of you?", Mrs. Garvin asked. Two more heads nodded.

Then a young woman, pulling her maroon coat more tightly about her, spoke. Her words came slowly and her eyes shifted here and there without looking at anyone.

"You know, I find that it is very easy to come close to being brutal to my deaf boy", She hesitated for a long moment.

"It's so different from our boy who isn't deaf. I just can't communicate with Jeff. I ask him to do something, like 'put your pajamas on now. I pick up the pajamas and *show* him what I want done. I ask again. He balks. Then if this is the tenth time during the day I've had to go through this routine, I've had it! I'll grab him and force his pajamas on. Then he'll start kicking and twisting and biting and fighting like an animal. And when I spank him, if he's twisting and kicking. I'm liable to miss and hit him across the back or even on the face. I feel so bad, but what can I do?"

She looked down at her hands, clenched white against the deep maroon of her coat. She was fighting back tears of remorse and anger. Behind her I could see a row of hooks on the wall where Lynn and the others hung their coats each day. A sweater still dangled from one hook, a pair of black rain boots lay on the floor. I could hear the voices from the other groups scattered around the large classroom. At the same time, it was as if we were looking through the window at ourselves, seeing with frightening clarity how we acted, observing the cause of our own increasingly frequent fights with Lynn.

"It's time for your bath", would lead directly to a kicking, screaming struggle all the way into the tub. Once in it, she refused to get out; splashing water all over us, she clung to the faucet. When we motioned and called her to dinner, she came but refused to climb into her chair or eat. It happened almost every day over something, but her war of resistance was constantly interspersed by delightful periods of truce when she spontaneously cooperated.

The small group of parents and Mrs. Garvin discussed the problem from several angles; all the solutions offered seemed like ones we had heard before. The questions then shifted to lip reading, to speech therapy, to difficulties someone had keeping his daughter wearing her hearing aid.

Then, almost without thinking, I asked it. I heard myself saying the words that haunted me for years.

The question we had pushed out of our minds, avoided, as if we didn't *want* to find the answer. Even as I spoke, I wondered why we had not asked this question when Lynn's deafness was first confirmed.

"How many deaf children *actually* learn to talk clearly and lip-read everything you say?" I looked at Mrs. Garvin.

"And how long does it *really* take?"

Mrs. Garvin remained silent for several seconds, then began hesitantly,

"I'm not sure what the exact figures are. In the past the record has not been good for children born deaf because they were five or six or seven years old before they started school. But now, with children beginning at age three and even earlier, I think we can expect good results.

"Maybe you have some statistics on this", she said, looking directly at Barbara Simmons.

"Well, the statistics are not too encouraging", Mrs. Simmons said,
shaking her head.

"The latest study indicates that only five or ten percent of all the children born deaf ever develop intelligible speech. It can take fifteen years and still be very difficult to understand them." A stillness had settled over our group as she spoke. Skeptical, I leaned forward in my chair.

"Nobody can learn to lip-read everything." She went on.

"A skilled lip-reader—and that's most often someone who learned to speak *before* going deaf—is lucky if he can understand one fourth of what is said."
There was a gasp from the young mother who had told us about spanking her son.

"You *don't mean* that deaf children who start school as young as ours turn out that poorly, do you?", she asked, incredulous.

"Yes", Barbara Simmons said matter-of-factly. "That includes children starting before the age of one year."

In the long uncomfortable silence that followed I thought to myself, Five or ten percent! How can that be? My thoughts raced back to the Jane Brooks School for the Deaf. I could see myself walking with Louise from one class to another, listening to the strange sounds of deafness, watching as second- and third-grade children struggled to gain control over their unused voices. Finally, breaking the silence, I turned to Mrs. Garvin and asked,

"Do you agree?", I could see I was not the only skeptic in the group; several others were frowning, shaking their heads in disbelief.

"I think Barbara Simmons is probably correct", Mrs. Garvin replied.

"I'm not sure what the exact numbers are. I've taught deaf children for a long time and after their first year of preschool, at least by the time they're five, I can pretty well tell whether they're going to develop intelligible speech. Most will never make it."

"Then what do you do with the five-years-old you're pretty sure

won't make it?" I asked, still doubting what I had heard.

Mrs. Garvin looked down at the floor, then back at the group.

"Well", she said slowly, "we can't be one hundred percent sure. We have to keep trying. When a child gets older, if they still can't communicate orally when they are in their teens, it's best to send that child to the state residential school."

Another strained silence ended when Dr. Mason asked the groups to break up and return to the rows of chairs in the front.

The only thing I remember about the rest of that meeting was what Mr. Hockett, the principal, said when he reported on the discussion that had taken place in his group.

"We talked about temper tantrums and what to do when your child absolutely refuses to obey", he began.

"Some of the parents in our group said that even spanking their child or sending him to his room did not bring cooperation. One parent suggested a solution that might help those of you who have similar difficulties."

"She had tried spanking. She had restricted her son 's activities. She took away privileges. And sometimes, at her wit's end, she just gave in to what the child wanted. One day another temper tantrum occurred. She had reached her limit, so when her son completely refused to obey, in desperation she grabbed him and forcibly shoved him in the shower. Then she turned on the cold water, clothes and all.

After half a minute, she turned off the shower, pulled him out and started drying him off. His temper tantrum had ended! She helped him change clothes and for the rest of the day he was most cooperative."

All the way home I kept thinking about our discussion group.

"Five or ten percent make it."

"I can pretty well tell by the time they're five whether they're going to develop intelligible speech."

Could she tell right now if Lynn was going to make it? Had we overlooked some hidden sign? "She's a phenomenal lip reader."

More than one of Lynn's teachers had described her that way. Was it possible that she *still* might not develop speech? How could anyone be sure at this age? Wasn't it worth it to keep trying?

Louise and I both wondered about the group of concerned parents who would meet at Sutter Hospital the next evening. Why would these people give up? Did most of them have older children? Had their children started too late?

At home, I paid Pat Kerns and then walked her down to her house. Light streamed from windows along Finsbury Avenue, casting dark shadows across the lawns on each side of the street.

Our house seemed especially quiet when I returned; Louise was sitting at the oak table in our small kitchen.

Steam rose in two thin columns from the coffee she had poured. I sat down, took a sip, put my cup back down on the table and sat for a long moment in silence.

"Tom", Louise finally said, "I don't think our situation looks good.

Lynn can't talk now and she might never talk. In fact, it seems to me that she has regressed since she started school this year!"

I sipped my coffee slowly, searching for words, reviewing the evidence, trying to sort out my own feelings.

"For the first time, I realized that we had worked so hard on speech and lip reading that we had never fully entertained the possibility of *failure*. I a few months.

Lynn would celebrate her fifth birthday. She could not talk; the few words she spoke were intelligible only to us and a few close friends. She could only lip-read names of common objects and a few common verbs. What if all our efforts, what if all Lynn's valiant attempts actually did fail? What then? What were the alternatives? Clothed in the enigmatic and forbidden phrases like 'manual language,' signs,' 'fingerspelling,' 'residential school,' 'deaf-and-dumb,' the alternatives conjured up animalistic, nonhuman images in my mind. I feared to think of them. I didn't want to investigate them as a possibility for Lynn.

For three years we had accepted the axiom: *all deaf children can learn to lip-read and talk almost as well as their hearing peers.* This axiom was conditional, we knew that. It required an early start and a pure oral environment, but we had not denied Lynn either of these conditions.

Now we had encountered contradictory evidence. Or maybe it was only hearsay. Surely, if 95 percent of deaf children *never* learned to talk well enough to communicate, those facts would have been reported in the *Journal of the Alexander Graham Bell Association.* I couldn't recall a single article or news item in the *Volta Review* that even hinted at such a possibility.

I got up from the table, poured more coffee into our cups and sat down.

"Well, what else can we do?", I asked, feeling perturbed at Louise for her questions, at myself for entertaining doubts.

"We can't just give up and send her off to the residential school! If she's ever going to get an education, a good job, have a family of her own—she has to learn to live in a hearing world. That means we can't quit now! It's the day-to-day thing that's hard; I realize some days look like no progress. But I think Lynn's doing better than we think. Like the sleeping thing. Only a few months ago we thought she'd never learn."

Louise nodded, though I sensed her discouragement even as I struggled with my own. Lynn *had* finally learned to sleep through the night in her own bed.

For more than a year we had lived with her nightly visits, and the problem continued after we moved from Southern California to Sacramento.

Several times a week Lynn would come to our room in the middle of the night, roll out a sleeping bag next our bed and sleep there until morning.

"What can we do to help her sleep through?" We had both asked the question on many nights but the answer clued us.

Finally, after she had become familiar with our neighborhood and begun to enjoy school, we decided to make another attempt. We carried her back to bed, trying to explain what we wanted. On some nights, she slept through in her own room and this shored up our hope that it could become a permanent nighttime routine. On those rare mornings when we awoke to find her sleeping bag empty, we raced to her bedside, and with lavish praise, tried to impress on her the importance of her accomplishment. But our enthusiasm remained a mystery to her.

Then we hit upon a plan. I went into Lynn's room one evening after she had fallen asleep and took her picture. When the print came back, Louise pasted it to a blank calendar she had ruled out on a large piece of red construction paper. Lynn laughed and pointed to the picture as we attached it to her bedroom wall. The we began a bedtime ceremony of looking at the picture together, nodding our heads and pointing to Lynn.

"You can sleep in jour own bed all night. You're a big girl now."

A hint of understanding rose in her eyes.

"Louise! Lynn made it through the night!", I woke with a start. It must have been a week after we had hung the calendar in her bedroom; we both went to see if she had awakened. Louise retrieved the box of gold stars from the top of the refrigerator and when Lynn opened her eyes, we were both standing next to her bed exuding approval.

"You slept in your own bed!" Louise exclaimed and gave Lynn a warm hug. We took her to the calendar and with great fanfare recorded the accomplishment. Louise gave her a gold star and pointed to the first square on the numberless calendar below the photograph of Lynn sleeping. Lynn couldn't have looked more pleased as she licked the star and pasted it in place.

For the next twenty-seven days Lynn slept through the night in her own bed and woke each morning to add another gold star under her picture.

When the calendar filled up, we left it hanging on her wall. We half expected a return to the old pattern, but night after night she stayed in her bed until the picture calendar grew old and was unceremoniously replaced by a picture Lynn had painted in school.

We had stumbled onto the solution which, in hindsight, appeared so simple. I wondered about the problems that still remained. We desperately needed to talk to Lynn in words she could understand.

To have her communicate in words *we* could understand. We longed for a common language to handle the common routines of dressing, taking a bath, cleaning up her room, coming in, going out, waiting in the car, going back to find her coat, taking turns in children's games, and a hundred others.
Would we have to find a different solution for each of these while we waited for her tongue to be loosened?

One evening a few days after Thanksgiving, Louise came across a notice in the local paper. A group which called themselves the Concerned Parents of Starr King Exceptional School had presented a proposal to the San Juan Board of Education. They asked for a class in which the teacher used sign language in addition to speech, because their children were not learning to speak and lip-read at a rate which allowed adequate communication at home. The article pointed out that Starr King school did not teach sign language to deaf children, nor allow them to use it at the school.

"Do you suppose they are the same group of parents who announced that meeting at Sutter Hospital a couple of weeks ago?", I asked after Louise read the article.

"I still can't understand why they want to use sign language with such young children. We probably have as much trouble communicating with Lynn as they do with their kids. I don't know.

The next couple of years are crucial. I don't want to ruin Lynn's chances of learning to talk by admitting failure now when she just might start talking in the next year or two."
Three years later Lynn came home from school with several mimeographed notices. One was on the table with the new *Volta Review* which had arrived in the mail. The large blue printing which spread out across the entire page of the notice caught my attention.

ORALISM VS. MANULISM

ALL PARENTS OF STARR KING EXCEPTIONAL SCHOOL ARE INVITED
TO AN IMPORTANT MEETING TOMORROW NIGHT WHERE WE WILL
DISCUSS THE CONTROVERSY OVER ORALISM AND MANUALISM AND
HOW IT WILL AFFECT THE SCHOOL.
TIME 7.30
ALL PARENTS URGED TO ATTEND.

I picked up the *Volta Review* and sat down to browse through it.

It was the December 1969 issue. The table of contents listed an article on special education in Sweden, another on the mental health of deaf children. I turned the page and quickly scanned an advertisement:

'Electronic Futures, Inc. A wireless auditory training system.'

I turned another page.

Book reviews. The first title caught my attention. The Influence of Finger Spelling on the Development of Language Communication and Educational Achievement in Deaf Children, by Steven P. Quigley, Ph.D.

The review is written by the director of Tucker-Maxon Oral School.

Dr. Quigley had studied two hundred students in six public residential schools to determine which method worked best: a pure oral approach or an oral approach that also used finger spelling. According to Quigley, his study showed that the use of finger spelling improved school performance and communicative skills among deaf children.

However, the reviewer disagreed. Carefully and systematically he pointed out that Dr. Quigley had made a number of questionable assumptions. The superior performance by children using finger spelling might also be attributable to the fact at a residential school, whatever approach used can be monitored and controlled more easily. The control groups who used a pure oral approach had not lived in such an environment.

Clearly, the study didn't stand up under careful scrutiny. It appeared that Dr. Quigley wanted to prove that finger spelling worked better than a pure oral approach. I was glad someone could refute these kinds of claims and wondered if the group of Concerned Parents at Starr King ever read the *Volta Review*.

The next evening when I left home alone to go to the parents' meeting, I picked up the December *Volta Review*. I wasn't prepared to speak up the meeting, but if the debate over the oral and manual approach should become heated. I could at least cite these arguments against the use of finger spelling for young children.

I pulled into the driveway of Starr King Exceptional School; more than the usual number of cars were parked in the asphalt-covered lot. I decided to sit near the back; if the meeting became uninteresting.

I could slip out early and go home.

Chapter 17

I left the car and walked quickly up a roadway that ran parallel to a long classroom. It led to the Special Education offices and the classrooms on Starr King campus. The lights from several office windows cast yellow streaks and dark shadows across the grass and covered circular drive, where each morning the buses discharged their load of handicapped children.

More than a dozen rows of brown metal chairs had been unfolded and arranged in the middle of a large meeting room that functioned during the day as lunchroom and gymnasium.

Already more than half had been taken and people were moving into vacant rows. Lunch tables lined the back wall and in one corner a trampoline stood folded up near a pile of tumbling mats.

Several groups of parents and teachers had collected near the front of the room and stood talking. I recognized a few faces but, as yet,

I did not know anyone on a first-name basis. Lynn's teacher had taken a seat in the third row; Mr. Hockett moved among the groups, welcoming parents to the meeting with a broad smile and handshakes. Wishing Louise had come with me, I made a beeline for the table against the back wall which would give me a good view of the room. I looked casually at my watch as I sat on the edge of a corner table near the rear exit. Seven twenty-five. The meeting would begin in five minutes.

Then I saw them! Their hands darting in and out, fingers pointing, twisting, jabbing the air lightning strokes. At least a dozen of them had taken chairs together, several rows in front of me, slightly off to one side. One woman, her chair turned around to face the others, wove patterns in the air with her hands as she spoke each word silently. A curious feeling came over me, as if I were in a foreign country, unable to speak the native language. Judging by the glances of curiosity from parents around the room, I knew that others felt this same mood of apprehension.

The huddled groups engaged in conversation looked as if they were discussing the small band of deaf people. Obviously not parents or teachers, they seemed like intruders. As if by commons agreement, the hands of the deaf people fell silent. They turned to watch a large middle-aged man at the end of the row. A conspicuous plastic receiver protruded from one ear, the gray cord disappearing inside his shirt collar. He spoke with both hands to the woman who interpreted, his nimble fingers curling, knitting, jabbing and pointing in the small space before his chest, occasionally touching his head or chin.

I could catch expressions of interest here and there on half-turned faces, smiles, nods. His hands stopped and fell silent into his lap. All eyes shifted to the interpreter; people nodded in agreement as she said something with her hands and mouthed the words.

When she finished, the man with the hearing aid burst into a loud crackling laughter that sounded peculiarly 'deaf.' Everywhere around the multipurpose room, heads turned to look; the other deaf visitors smiled or laughed quietly, then continued their silent conversation, unaware of the attention briefly turned their way.

"Will everyone please take a seat now?", Mr. Hockett had gone to the front. Slowly the conversation died down. People in the back moved into the empty rows, someone went for more chairs, which squeaked loudly as they were unfolded.

"We're glad so many of you joined us tonight. This is an important meeting for all of us." He shifted from one foot to another, waiting for the talking to end.

"As you all know, Starr King Exceptional School has always been a *pure oral* school. In fact, for the last fourteen years, the San Juan Unified School District has always had a policy to maintain a pure oral environment in the special-education programs for the hearing-impaired."

I listened to Mr. Hockett, but my eyes kept shifting back to the woman who continued to interpret for the deaf visitors. The designs created by her hands flowed with incredible speed.

"We think that Starr King has one of the best programs in the United States. Most parents are pleased with the progress that their children have made here. It is my impression from talking with many of you that most parents want their children to have an oral education."

"A few parents, the ones who call themselves Concerned Parents, have gone to the board about starting classes using manual communication. However, many feels that our school should remain a *pure* oral school. The deaf people who learn the manual language do not have the same advantages in a hearing world. They can obtain poor jobs. They live in the deaf ghetto. They miss out on many things that hearing people enjoy. Tonight, we are here to discuss this request made to the board."

The interpreter's gestures involved both hands, sweeping, integrated patterns that moved in a kind of silent musical rhythm. Then, in the midst of these patterns, she would stop and make tiny jerking movements with her fingers of one hand.

I noticed other parents glancing uncomfortably in the direction of the deaf, then studiously trying to ignore this new phenomenon that had invaded our parent group meeting. "These *concerned* parents", Mr. Hockett looked quickly at several parents sitting with the deaf visitors, "their proposal to the Board of Education asks for teachers to instruct their children in sign language. Mrs. Simmons will read that request so you will all be aware of what they want in our program. Then I think we can discuss it. It does involve *all* the children in our district."

Barbara Simmons walked to the front of the room. She began to read from a sheaf of papers in her hands:
We are the parents of bilingual hearing-impaired children. Our children are not only using the spoken language but the language of *signs*. We are here not as parents with a quarrel with any teacher, administrator, or any other parents. Instead, we respect those who possess differing views and we would hope that they would grant us the right to differ.

There will be those who will say that our children should be kept at Starr King but stop their use of signs. As our children become more proficient in the use of signs and are better able to communicate with their friends, it will become increasingly difficult to stop the signs without having to use some of the methods that a few teachers have mentioned.

Besides the usual slapping of hands, there is the use of nylon stockings to tie the children's hands behind their back, and some oral schools use bags in which they place the offenders' hands and then tie it. Even though the teachers were not to instigate such action, our children will be made to feel that they are inferior by their peer group. Many of the oral parents have drilled into their children that to sign is bad. We can understand why these parents have done this. But it will not make our children feel welcome in that type of school environment.

She read the requests for special classes, folded the papers together and returned to her seat. The requests she made all sounded reasonable. And even though she had asked for classes using sign language, she had also emphasized they still wanted oral language for their children.

Mr. Hughes, the PTA president, went to the front of the group.
All whispering had ceased, although I noticed one deaf woman gesturing to a man sitting next to her.

"We are concerned parents too!"

Mr. Hughes gripped the edge of the table and looked directly at the small group of parents sitting with deaf people. His tense voice filled the large room.

"I don't think it was right for you to make your *request* to the Board of Education without notifying the rest of us that we could tell them of *our* concerns. We have deaf children too!"

Heads nodded around the room. The woman interpreting for the deaf visitors seemed unmoved by the comment, her fingers picked up speed as she changed the spoken words into signs.

"We believe that our deaf children have the right to teach them a *mother tongue!* Sign language is not even a language!"

With each sentence Mr. Hughes's voice crept to a higher pitch.

"It's just a primitive form of gesturing! I don't know why they even call it sign *language!* If you teach deaf children those gestures, they will never learn to talk. They will never learn anything! You can't teach them to read and write using that sort of thing!"

The interpreter maintained a steady rhythm, painting Mr. Hughes's words in the air. It did seem that some of her movements had grown more exaggerated, as if to match the deep feelings conveyed by his words.

Mr. Hughes paused, looked down, then went on in a quieter tone, "I'll never forget" -he shook his head slowly- "an experience I had some years ago. I was a life-insurance salesman. I went to this one house and knocked on the door; the lady let me come in. A young man in his early twenties was sitting there. It became very apparent to me that something was wrong with him."

"Is your son deaf?", I finally asked.

"Oh, yes. He's been deaf since birth."

"Can he talk?"

"No, he can't talk."

"That young man would try to talk with his mother, but he could only make the most grotesque sounds you ever heard. It sounded like an animal! Then he would move his hands trying to communicate, gesturing, pointing, as if he wanted something. His mother would go get it. They seemed to partially understand each other, but it was really awful."

He paused for a moment.

"It was the gestures that had kept him from learning how to talk. And I just determined right there that my daughter should learn how to speak.

We would never use those gestures that had prevented this deaf kid from learning to talk. And another thing … "

He glanced in the direction of the deaf visitors.

"If we have a manual class for some kids at Starr King, even if they go to another school, our kids will see them signing on the bus and begin to sign themselves. It will spread and we will no longer have a pure oral school. The rest of us are happy with it as it is. If you want your children to learn to sign instead of talk, why don't you send them to the state residential school."

Mr. Hughes stopped for a moment, then suggested we open the meeting to discussion with another parent. Eager hands went up all over the room except for the silent group of deaf visitors.

"I don't want my child exposed to these gestures", said one woman.

"If some parents have given up, that's their business, but I think we should keep Starr King a pure oral school", added a young-looking gray-haired man with glasses.

"My boy is four years old. I'll admit that communication at home isn't always easy. But he *does* lip-read. Someday I'm sure he'll start talking.
I think we have to be patient. I'm just glad the teachers and the administrations at Starr King are so willing to work with us to teach our kids to talk."

A slight woman in a blue coat, she went on to praise the school as one of the best she had known.

The deaf visitors watched the woman interpreter change the various comments into signs; they looked first to the parent or teacher who spoke, then back to her rapidly changing hands. More than one person talked about the John Tracy Clinic, the research it had done on deaf kids, and that if sign language worked, surely those people would know about it.

I began to feel that nearly all the opinions weighed against the concerned parents and their request for change. Then a woman in her late thirties got to her feet. Her blond hair fell close against her narrow, attractive face. She waited until recognized, then started hesitantly,

"I'd like to say something about our daughter, Debbie. She's probably older than most of your children. For ten years we have hoped that she would talk, patiently struggling to communicate as best we could. Debbie's almost twelve now. And most of that time we wondered what was wrong, if maybe she was retarded."

"We were told again and again: Keep trying. You must have patience. Debbie can lip-read and someday she'll talk."

"I'm afraid we were patient. Too patient. We waited too many years before we gave up! Thank God for Mr. Wilson, that he taught at Starr King. He has deaf parents and he can sign and he understands deaf children better than anyone else. Last summer he started a class for six of the deaf children here at Starr King, children everyone considered failures. Debbie was one of those failures!" Her eyes dropped to the floor momentarily; hardly anyone or anything moved in the entire room except for the hands of the interpreter.

"Well, he started a class at Cameron Ranch School using sign language along with speech. What a difference it has made with our daughter! Now my husband and I are learning sign language too, and for the first time we can communicate with Debbie. She can talk to us with her hands. What's more, first time she's learning things in school.
I think these parents have made a very reasonable request. They just want a class at a different school with a teacher who can add signs to speech.
These parents want to start *now,* while their children are young. I wish we had started when we first discovered our daughter was deaf."

When she sat down I could see her husband lean over and whisper something to her. For a long minute, no one said anything.

The Mr. Hughes asked if anyone else wished to speak. A woman in a green pants suit stood up, an angry expression on her face. Her voice cracked with emotion.

"We have *two* deaf children", She paused as if to allow the enormity of their problem to sink in. "We lived in a small town in Iowa, where they had almost nothing for handicapped children in the schools. We decided that if our children were to get an education, we would have to move, so we started looking at programs all over the country. We wanted a pure oral program, one where they could learn to speak and lip-read."

"We located some good schools, ones that provided excellent oral classes, but they almost always had classes in signs for the older children who had failed. We knew that if we sent our children to those schools, they would pick up signs from these other children. It could have kept them from even learning to talk. Finally, we settled on Starr king because it had a first-rate oral program. My husband had to quit a good job; we moved to Sacramento; he had to search for another job and take a cut in pay. But it was worth it! One of our children has some speech and we manage to communicate. The other one can't say a word yet and maybe will need signs someday. But we feel we must give our one child the chance to become oral, to allow him to live in a hearing world. That's why we came to this school!"

Her voice had become louder and louder as she spoke.

"Now, *we* had to give up a lot to put our children in Starr King, to have a pure oral school. If a few parents have decided to have their children learn sign language, that is *their* choice. But why can't they move to another location? Why can't they find a school that already uses signs? I don't think it's right for them to try to change a program that other parents believe in and have made great sacrifices to make it available to their children."

I felt sorry for the woman as she sat down. I kept thinking about her one deaf child who could *not* speak. How would these two deaf brothers communicate with each other?

No one else from the Concerned Parents group had spoken. Couldn't they defend their request to the Board of Education? Why didn't anyone argue for adding sign language to the oral method? The sentiment at the meeting was obviously strongly in favor of the pure oral approach.

Although I agreed, I had begun to feel that some of those who defended Starr King's present program overstated the dangers of having one class that used sign language in addition to speech. Then a new hand went up: the deaf man with the hearing aid. Mr. Hughes pointed in his direction, he stood up and faced the audience while still in full view of the other deaf visitors. Everyone watched expectantly.

"I would like to say something", he began in a loud voice that had a noticeable accent. If he had not signed or worn a hearing aid, I would have assumed he was a foreigner. Yet his words came clear and unmistakable.

"Some of the things I've been hearing tonight are *ridiculous!"* He shook his head, looked around the room, and at the same time moved his hands in rhythm with his words.

"You people don't know what you're talking about! I *am* deaf! My hearing aid does *not* help me. I wear it for only one reason: it makes people talk slower and then I can lip-read more of what they say. I would *prefer* to communicate with everyone in signs but, of course, that's not possible. Even though I have speech and can lip-read some people, on my job I always rely on writing to make sure I am understood and that I understand what others say.

"Now I want to ask all of you one question. Is there anybody here who can't understand me?"

He looked all around the room, slowly moving his eyes from one row to the next. A strange silence hung over the audience, as if transfixed by hearing this man speak. Not a single hand went up.

"Do you know why I can talk? Because I was *not born* deaf! I could hear until I was six years old. Then I went deaf. I didn't have to go through a long period of learning to make each little sound that I could *not* hear."

" Most of your children will never have that advantage and they will *never talk* as well as I do even if they spend all their life working on it. Now I want to say one other thing. Sign language has not ruined my speech. Before I learned sign language, I had a difficult time understanding what people said. Tonight, I followed every word that was spoken because this hearing person interpreted for me in sign language."

He pointed toward the woman. As he spoke, his hands continued their rapid pace of movements.

"There's been an attack made on sign language tonight. That it's not even a language. I don't think this gentleman who spoke knows anything about sign language. Do you know a single sign? It's a perfectly good language and I've been able to understand everything that was said—not because I lip-read, but because this interpreter has used *sign language* to tell me what's going on. And that young man you referred to who couldn't talk, who could only point and try to make his mother understand what he wanted—if his parents had known sign language, if he had known sign language, that could never have happened.

He was that way *because* of your pure oralist approach. He had grown up without *any* means of communication!

"If your children knew sign language, they could easily grasp what you or their teachers wanted to communicate. Of course, you would have to learn sign language first. But is that too much to ask of parents with deaf children and professionals who work with the deaf?

Most of your children who are deaf will need sign language to help them get an education. And sign language will help their speech too. And it won't put them in the 'deaf ghetto', wherever that is."

He looked in Mr. Hockett's direction, then added,

"I don't know where the deaf ghetto is, but if I live in it, that's okay by me. I drive a car, I have a pretty good job, I live in an expensive house. If that's living in the deaf ghetto, then it's the deaf ghetto!"

With that, he sat down amid the silent approving expressions from the other deaf visitors. I was deeply moved. His words rang in my ears:

"Your children need sign language." This stranger had lived with deafness. Other parents were talking now, but I heard none of them.

I looked down at the copy of the *Volta Review* I had brought to the meeting, folded it up and stuck it in my coat pocket. I no longer knew what to make of the article that criticized Dr. Quigley's research on using both oral and manual approaches. I had seen deaf people signing, talking, participating on an equal basis with the hearing world *because* of sign language, not in spite of it. I looked around the room at the teachers. They had special training in the education of the deaf, but none were deaf. I looked at the principal. He had talked about Starr King having one of the best programs in the United States, and the deaf who use manual language ending up in the deaf ghetto, but what, really, did he know of other deaf programs, of deaf ghettos? Not one adult at Lynn's school knew how to communicate with these deaf people in their language. None of them, so far as I knew, were deaf. I thought about Louise and me. We had no deaf friends. We knew nothing about the day-to-day lives of honest-to-God deaf adults.

What had happened? Why had our lives been so insulated from deaf adults? We had never heard the kind of things this deaf man said. The only deaf adults we knew of we read about in the

Volta Review. The Oral Deaf Adults. But surely there were thousands and thousands of others who graduated from state residential schools – the ones who had tried to learn to speak and had failed.

Had we been fooled into thinking that most deaf people learned to lip-read and speak so well that they became socially invisible, that they somehow melted into the larger hearing world and became one of 'us'? Could it be true that 90 percent of the deaf did not develop intelligible speech?

The deaf who had come tonight were certainly not Oral Deaf Adults. They lived by the language of signs, even though some could talk. I knew I had to find out more.

The meeting ended and I made my way through the milling crowd of parents to Barbara Simmons at the front.

"Hi, my name is Tom Spradley."

I had waited until she finished signing to one of the deaf visitors.

"You might remember me from the discussion group a couple weeks ago?"

"Sure, you have a little girl. In kindergarten, isn't she?"

"Yes. Lynn. She's profoundly deaf." Trying to sound neutral, I went on, "Your comments tonight were quite interesting. You seem to have a whole different slant on deafness and the education of deaf children. It's one I've never read about or heard of before."

"Well, yes, I guess not everyone agrees with it."

She smiled and let her eyes sweep over the dispersing crowd of parents who had broken into many small groups, some huddled in serious talk about the discussion that had ended.

"Where can I get more information about the kind of thing you we're talking about?"

"Would you like to bring your family and come over to our house next week? You could meet some of our deaf friends. You could learn a lot from them. And I can also give you copies of some current research articles about deaf children and deaf adults."

Even as I accepted Barbara's invitation, wrote down her address and made my way out of the meeting room, I had second thoughts. Had I given her the *wrong* impression?

Did we really want to get involved with this sign-language thing, even to spend the time finding out about it? And who were her 'deaf friends'? What would they be like? Would they pressure us to start Lynn using gestures the way they did? Would we become involved in the controversy that had developed at Starr King?

That night when I arrived home Louise and I talked for several hours. I recounted the meeting in detail, describing the deaf visitors, the reactions of Mr. Hughes and several other parents, my impressions of the interpreter, and what the deaf man had said.

"Tom, I think we have to go very carefully", Louise had listened perceptively to my report of the evening.

"Lynn may not be making the fast progress we thought she would, but we've got her whole future to think about."

Then, in a voice that seemed to drift back to the past, Louise asked a sad tone, "Do you remember that deaf man in Oklahoma, the one I meet in the supermarket?"

I nodded, and we both knew instantly each other's thoughts. We had to make sure Lynn's future didn't turn out like that. It had happened a few weeks before we left Norman. I had driven Louise to the Safeway market a few blocks from our apartment on a scorching day when the humidity left everything damp and sticky.

I waited in the car; Louise had only a few grocery items to pick up, Lynn, always eager to go shopping, went along and climbed into the seat in the market basket. They started down the first aisle together, Lynn pointed to the bright packages and looked for other children, Louise was preoccupied with her list of things to buy.

Without warning, a large man in a threadbare sports coat loomed up in front of her basket, silently blocking the way. He pushed a card in front of Louise; it was pinned to a tiny handmade doll. The card said: "*I am deaf. Would you make a contribution?*"

Louise stared at the card. Glanced down at Lynn, back at the man, then began searching through her purse. All she could find was her checkbook.

"I am *really* sorry! I don't have any money! My daughter is deaf too."
She spoke slowly, her voice quivering, hoping the man could read her lips.
"How did you become deaf?"

Nervously the deaf man shifted from one foot to the other. He looked blankly at Louise through thick glasses. He wore a faded sweat shirt; beads of perspiration stood out on his forehead, wrinkled in confusion. Then he slowly reached into his pocket and took out a dirty pad of paper and a short stubby pencil. He started scribbling something, then handed it to Louise.

"*Deaf me. Chicken pox. Not hear.*"

"*I am sorry*", Louise scribbled hurriedly. "*My daughter was born deaf.*

I had German measles."

She handed the note pad back to the man, who stared at it for several seconds. A woman with a bandana around her head pushed a shopping basket past and looked curiously at the two of them trying to communicate.

A smile spread across the man's face, then he began writing again, this time more eagerly: "*I deaf too.*"

He pointed at Lynn, then at his ears. "*I go to Sulphur, the state school for deaf.*"

133

"I am sorry. I don't have any money", Louise written back, then awkwardly moved off down the aisle as she watched him take this doll and hold it out to another shopper. She finished quickly, went to the express lane and wrote a check for the amount of purchase. As she lifted Lynn out of the basket and started to pick up the bag of groceries, she saw the man shuffling out the door into the parking lot.

I could tell by Louise's hurried walk that something was wrong. She came directly to my window. Fighting back the tears, she spoke in urgent, anxious tones.

"Tom, quick! Give me a dollar bill. Quick!"

I reached for my wallet. "It's for a deaf man." I handed her the money and opened the door to help Lynn into the back seat. Louise turned and ran across the parking lot to an old Chevrolet, the front bumper missing, the right fender rusted and crumpled. I could see two men sitting in the car. Louise went to the passenger side and pushed the dollar bill to the man she had met.

"No, you keep the doll, sell it to somebody else", she said when he held it out to her. Then she turned and walked quickly back to the car.

For days after that we talked about this deaf man. Where had he come from? What kind of education had he received at the state school in Sulphur? Already, at three and a half, Lynn seemed to have progressed further than this adult. He confirmed everything we had heard about the state residential school.

He couldn't speak! That bothered us the most. How different from the Oral Deaf Adults we had read about. How different from Carolyn Graves at the Jane Brooks oral school in Chickasha. We felt a deep sadness for this man, and at the same time, a sense of hope for Lynn. But tonight, I had seen another deaf man. I had heard him speak. Yet this man had also used sign language at the same time. It had been deeply unsettling.

134

Perhaps he was a special case. He had lost his hearing at age six, after learning to talk. Perhaps children like Lynn who had been born deaf required more insulation from sign language.

We need more information. More facts.

Several roads fanned out in front of us. All seemed to hold great risks for Lynn. We fell asleep long after midnight, anxious and troubled about the future

15. The Poster on the Wall

Somewhere in a large office building, a beautifully colored poster is hanging on a brick wall. It depicts the windmills of the village Kinderdijk in Holland. Because I work in that building, I sit right in front of it. In the last fifteen minutes of my work time, I often look with attention at this "painting." In the picture you see the freshly painted windmills, the deep blue water and the light green reeds. It's a proper Dutch landscape in the middle of a canal, with an island full of reeds; it seems to float.

When I look at the poster all alone in the office room, I suddenly get the feeling that someone is standing next to my chair. Turning around I see a heavy, hairy head. A remarkable sense of recognition grows within me. It is Rembrandt van Rijn standing here! Before I get a chance to look at him more closely, I see his paint-covered finger point to the poster. I can see his mouth moving, but I cannot understand him because of the abundant hair growth around his lips. I shrug. What he says cannot be understood. The eyes of the world-famous painter sparkle with anger. I notice it and offer him my apology and let him know that I cannot understand him. He hears me and shakes his mighty head. He does not understand me, I think. I hasten to tell him that I am completely deaf. Because there are quite a few office pieces lying on my desk in a scanty manner, Rembrandt resolutely takes a sheet of blank paper from my desk. I see his hand making impatient movements. Ah, he certainly wants a pen or something, I think, a little shocked. Hastily but reverently, I hand him a blue marker. But he shakes his head, while his eyes search the surface of the desk. Oh, I think, he was expecting to get a goose quill. Without fear I take the pen off the table and write as clearly as possible, "Rembrandt."

He looks at me for a long time, walks past me and sits down in a chair. A moment later he pushes the sheet of paper under my nose. With great difficulty, I read his 17th-century handwriting: he wants to know who did the painting on the wall. It is so beautifully painted.

Now I am faced with the great difficulty of explaining to the painter that it is not a painting, but a photographic reproduction.

Of course, I try to explain on paper how it works, but he is not interested in what I write. It could also be that my handwriting is difficult for him to decipher; I notice this from the shaking of his head and the swinging motion of his hand. On the paper he repeats his question about who the maker of this "painting" is. Helplessly, I shrug my shoulders and write that I cannot hear at all. To my surprise, Rembrandt writes more clearly this time, "Deaf and dumb?"

"Yes, I am deaf, but not dumb. I can speak."

He looks at me for a long time with a surprised look. On the paper I read what he writes next. "I do not think you're deaf."

"Oh no. Why?" I try to say as intelligibly as possible.

Rembrandt shakes his head violently and writes with graceful strokes, "A deaf and dumb man like you should beg on the street with a bell in his hand, but you have nice clothes and you work here. No, I do not think you're deaf."

While I write on a new piece of paper that I've been to school and learned a lot, Rembrandt looks long and carefully at the poster. Then he snatches the paper from my hand and writes, "That's a very good painting!"

I nod and want to say something, but Rembrandt is suddenly gone.

I am back in the present. Smiling, I look at the poster.

There is a world between Rembrandt's and the present. Then, skillful painters made beautiful portraits and landscapes of the Netherlands, and society did not know how to make contact with deaf people who had no education. Now, there are many technical ingenuities and good opportunities for deaf people in society.

16.   Surdiopolis, the Deaf City

Eliza Mistinquet is special; she was born seven seconds after the turn of the 21st century, so on the first of January of the year 2001. In this story, she is a lot older and she is now a sociologist by profession.

One day at her workplace she is staring outside. Her roe-like eyes do not really see the high silhouette of steel outside that is so famous. She thinks back to a remark her father made when she was visiting her home last night. He claimed that more and more deaf people are emigrating to Surdiopolis. She too wants to do so and she wonders what Louis, her deaf-born husband, thinks about that. Nothing could be seen on his face last night. It seemed that it was slipping past him. It may well be that he has no interest in the deaf city. Tonight, I will ask him how he feels about it, she decides. I know, after all, that he loves his birthplace a lot: Paris with all its history and monumental buildings. And, she wonders, would our children be allowed to Surdiopolis too?

When Eliza comes home late in the afternoon, she finds her husband with a newspaper in the living room. She walks to the sideboard, which dates from the last century, and takes the pile of mail. Before she gets the chance to look at it, she is disturbed by her eldest daughter who has just come home. After a short meal, consisting only of large food pills and a delicious dessert, Eliza tells Louis and the three children that she would like to go to her hobby room. She tells them she has something she wants to think about. Her husband is used to her doing this and nods. In her room she sits comfortably in an easy chair, and she reads a report in the magazine for the Deaf that came in the mail. Yes! There you have it, she thinks. Highly interesting. Almost every day there is news about the new city. By walking along the wall, the television screen comes on. On the remote control, she then taps in the teletext number. Yes, there is something about the enchanting city. Many more deaf experts are needed to further expand this city.

Eliza looks thoughtfully ahead. Could the city need her? In 'd'Echo,' her office, her hearing colleagues do not know what she needs: good cooperation and pleasant communication.

In Surdiopolis, things are definitely done very differently; she would like and could have a leading position there. She grabs the latest edition of the encyclopedia of Gallaudet Press University from the shelves. There she finds a summary of the reasons for the foundation of Surdiopolis. Curious and also emotionally involved she reads:

The rights of the deaf people and their organizations, such as the right to own identity, culture, and history are hardly developed in many countries because of incomprehensible opposition from their governments. Even worse, many governments also encourage the inclusion of the organizations of the deaf in a disabled framework, even in highly civilized countries.

The recognition of Sign Language as the natural language of the Deaf comes up against a wall of ignorance and refusal in many countries.

The oral method is still used in many countries in deaf education instead of the superior sign language.

The early identification of deafness and the assistance to hearing and/or deaf parents still leaves a lot to be desired in many countries.

In some countries, the speech method is still used in education rather than sign language. This method stops the further intellectual development of the pupils at schools for deaf children.

The cochlear implantation for children born deaf and children deafened at a later age is mandatory in many countries.

The advice of Deaf people is still ignored, for example, the proposal for the introduction of bilingual education, deaf teachers, and the culture of the Deaf in the Deaf Education.
Deaf youth gets few opportunities to participate fully in vocational education since there is a lack of a good supply of interpreters.

Eliza's breath escapes with an outraged hiss. That's how it is! She nods fiercely. She suddenly realizes how logical it is that the establishment of the deaf city was preceded by protests inspired by the famous "Deaf President Now" protest in the last century at Gallaudet University in Washington DC. Eliza blames herself that she had no interest in such matters then. She thinks that they can use her talents and commitment in Surdiopolis better than in Paris.

Eliza reads about the tough opposition from the governments of many countries that the board of the World Federation of the Deaf and other people have experienced. The board convened an extra meeting on a memorable day and appointed a special committee. This committee, consisting of people from five continents, often met at a distance via the multifunctional Videophone connection.

During the last meeting where everyone was together, the committee members needed a few days to refine the final report. The result was great, but the execution was delayed for a long time due to all kinds of circumstances. And then suddenly came the day that they succeeded.

The board of the World Federation of the Deaf recognized that the financial problem had to be tackled on a large scale. It did not intend, for example, to hold collections or to request subsidies from the United Nations. The board only invited a few deaf billionaires to discuss how things should be dealt with. They secretly met in the Waldorf Astoria Hotel in New York.

There the decision was made that a deaf city was to be built on Earth. Some of the sugar daddies initially did not like the idea of a brand-new city. They were so tight that they would rather keep their money in an old sock. Fortunately, the board of the federation knew how to persuade people and then they felt better, freed from the idea that only the possession of a lot of money would make them happy. But they only realized this when the deaf city was actually built out of the dreams of idealistic and practical deaf people.

In a few years' time and with great speed, Surdiopolis was built in an area that used to consist only of sand. The temperature there had become more moderate over the past decades by a miraculous play of Mother Nature. As a result, fertile soil had been created, which meant that, yet unknown, edible plants, worked their way up to the surface.

Eliza slowly closes the tome. It's amazing! The young history of Surdiopolis resembles a repeat of previous times but is cast in a different form. Until 1952, there was a community of very smoothly gesticulating deaf and hearing people on Martha's Vineyard, the island off the North American coast. Eliza also remembers such a community somewhere in the interior of Mexico.

Eliza notices that the door next to her chair is slowly being opened. There is Madeleine, her eldest, waving her hand. Eliza raises her eyebrows questioningly. "Yes, what is it?"

"Mum, there's someone on the phone."

Eliza asks with her voice, "Who?"

"Grandpa," says Madeleine, while her mouth forms a playful smile.

In the living room, Eliza sees a figure on the screen and she says, "Hello, how are you and Mommy?"

"We're well, and you?"

Eliza sees her father asking her a question with his moving hands. "Have you also seen the report in the magazine about Surdiopolis?"

She makes the typical gesture with her fist that says "yes," by moving it up and down.

"There is great news about Surdiopolis again," says her father.

"Exactly, did you read it?"

Her father, with his typical wine-red cheeks, nods enthusiastically. "Say, Eliza, what do you think, shall we go and live in Surdiopolis?"

Eliza, however, asks with a worried face, "You are not going to move to the deaf city, are you?!"

Her father laughs and says that he cannot imagine that his wife and he himself would just leave Paris, but that they would like to go there on holiday.

"Oh, how long would you stay away for, do you think?"

"About ten days or so. We'll see."

"Yes, yes, very nice."

Suddenly, Eliza realizes she has a unique opportunity to get some advance impressions of Surdiopolis.

"When are you going?" asks Eliza with great interest.

"Well, we do not have a date yet…wait a minute, you talk so much, let me speak…I wanted to say, Mom and I have been thinking about whether you all like to join us. Maybe that would be fun for the kids."

Eliza is speechless with her hands and then reacts exuberantly: "Well, I love you, Daddy. Shall I tell Louis now?"

"Yes, do that. Please keep it brief; the phone is expensive," he gestures.

"Okay," says Eliza. "Can I call you tomorrow evening for the answer?"

"Of course."

After the usual greeting she pushes the off button on the phone screen, while inside of her an orchestra is playing. There, in Surdiopolis, is her chance!

The next day, two weeks before leaving for Surdiopolis, Eliza reads with increasing surprise the messages on the teletext about the massive emigration of deaf people from Ateland. Eliza has to rub her eyes and read it again. Yes, it really says so. Amazing. Together with her husband, she reads that 5,517 deaf people have left for Deaf Town in just one week. They could only do so when it became known that the emigration stop for Atelanders was lifted because of the favorable socio-economic situation.

Eliza laughs out loud and thinks it's a nice joke. Louis then says that he does not to understand why. His wife explains to him that the education of the deaf in Ateland, despite frequent protests by adult deaf people, continues to hold on to an oral method.

"Now almost all deaf adults are leaving Ateland!" Eliza concludes with emotion on her face. Louis nods and says that it really amazes him.

"Those so-called experts from the hearing community are so obstinate."

There is a silence between Eliza and Louis for a short while. Louis gets up and paces through the room.

"What's with you?" Eliza asks.

Louis then looks at his wife and laughs a bit. "In recent times, a lot has been published about Surdiopolis. It is remarkable, a

144

magical attraction for one planet, while it does not touch the other planet in any way."

"You do say that beautifully," laughs Eliza.

"So, what do you think of the deaf city? Does this city offer deaf people like us a solution to our problems with hearing people?" Louis asks with a tense look on his face.

Eliza, however, walks toward him with a relaxed face and puts her hands around his waist.

Louis asks, "What's with you? Don't you like the idea of going to Surdiopolis in about two weeks' time?"

Eliza suddenly feels her body vibrate. Only for joy, now that she knows that her husband would also like to go there. She takes a few steps backward to look at his face and says with full conviction, "Well, of course I do. I'd like to go there. My dear parents are giving us a great opportunity to orientate ourselves in that place."

Louis stares at her incredulously and slowly says, "I didn't expect that you would also like to go there."

Eliza smiles broadly. "How can you say that?"

"Uh, I just didn't think you'd want to go."

"Then you make a mistake, my psychologist."

Louis grabs her by the waist spontaneously and they circle around as they dance across the room. Their children, Madeleine, Dominique, her younger sister, and Jean, their youngest brother, come in in single file and keep quiet. Dominique taps her mother's hip with her hand. Eliza turns around in alarm and now sees the children.

"Oh, you shocked me," she says, wildly gesticulating.

"Oh," Madeleine replies. "Mom and Dad, we have…No, can we go outside for a bit?"

"What is it with you guys?" Louis asks. He notices from Dominique's face that something is up.

"Well, Marie has something new and we want to look at it."

Louis looks at Eliza and says, "Okay, but I'd like you to be back home at seven."

The heads of the children nod simultaneously. When they are out of their sight, Louis waves at his wife to attract her attention.

"Yes?"

"I am sure that I can make a contribution in the deaf city because they are lacking skilled professionals."

Eliza looks at her husband for a while and asks, "Do you mean that you will want to work there?"

"Well, of course. Paris has a surplus of psychologists. You know that."

"Yes, yes. Do you really dare to go to the deaf city? Would not you miss the history of Paris here?" Eliza asks.

"Well, we can still go here on holiday."

"It would be nice for you if Surdiopolis has something in store for you. And then, I could also get work there."

"Of course. Not that long ago I read that Surdiopolis also needs some sociologists. Or would you prefer to do something else?"

"Well, I do not know exactly. Maybe I would want to hold a management position there."

Louis answers, "Yes, that's possible. So, the project you're working on is not finished yet?"

"No, not at all," Eliza suddenly reacts violently. "There is still a lot to do because my colleagues think they know better. I am in charge here, but I only meet mocking eyes. Yes, it is still tolerable, but for how long?"

Louis laughs.

"There's always something with hearing people."

"You're right in that."

In January of the first year of the 2060s, the plane departs from the Charles de Gaulle Airport, which is located to the north of Paris. After many hours of flying, a screen comes on. It is reported that Surdiopolis is in sight. High above the earth Eliza stands up from her chair and looks through the window. Fortunately, it's sunny outside. As a result, Eliza can clearly see a silhouette of Deaf City. She is very enthusiastic and calls her husband with a tap on his shoulder.

"Look, I never saw anything so beautiful in my life!"

Louis moves next to his wife and sees it too. "Yes, beautiful!"

From above, the city looks surprisingly nice. Surdiopolis has seven districts and a few public gardens. Each district and each public park is in the form of a hand-spelled letter.

"I see 'E' and there, 'W'," Louis' fingers spell enthusiastically.

Before Eliza looks down again, she sees a warning light coming on. Oh, fasten the seat belt before landing. She sees to it that her children fasten their belts too.

Her eyes shine so beautifully that Louis notices it. He remembers having seen her eyes like that when they knelt before the altar of Notre-Dame in Paris at their wedding. He knows that Eliza feels very happy at that moment.

Louis taps on his wife's arm and asks, "Did you know about those neighborhoods in alphabet shapes?"

"No. I am very surprised. So beautiful!"

"Yes, that is true," her husband nods.

Before they realize it, the plane, silently and without any shocks, lands at Surdioport.

"Weird, I do not hear anything at all: no sound," Madeleine gestures to her mother.

"Hey, you're right. I do not feel anything either."

147

Louis laughs and comments, "Yes, no wonder, because that is one of the newest functionalities of the world's largest airplane."

In a quarter of an hour, the passengers, mostly hearing tourists from America, leave the plane. After walking through the long gangway, they end up on a platform painted sea-green. There, someone from the customs department gestures—to the surprise of the families Hinault and Mistinquet.

"Passports, please."

Eliza looks at the young man for a while and gestures to Louis, "A nice start to our vacation."

The man glances through the documents and gestures: "Do you have anything to declare?"

Louis suddenly looks happy and says, "Our sign language!"

The young man bursts out laughing and gestures, "Okay."

The conversation between the two men takes less than half a minute, thanks to the sign language without limits. Eliza recognizes that the customs man uses American Sign Language (ASL) and that this could be the language of Surdiopolis. If so, it is a piece of cake for her husband.

A little later, the bus drives through different neighborhoods to the center of the city almost without any sound being felt by the family. When they are about to leave the bus, they read a warning sign in English on the footboard, "Just wait." Eliza is surprised and suddenly feels that she and the others are slowly moving downwards. Ah, the footboard moves down to the level of the pavement.

"Very useful, isn't it?" Eliza says dreamily. Louis has to wake her up from her reverie.

"Get out!"

"Yes, yes. It is beautiful here, don't you think?" she mimics with her face.

Out on the street, Louis notices that they have gotten off at the wrong stop. A female pedestrian suddenly appears at the corner of Henri Daniel Guyot Road, who, however, unintentionally shows her back. Eliza sees Madeleine calling, but the woman does not respond at all. Strange. But then it dawns on Eliza that the woman must also be deaf and she bursts out laughing. "Madeleine, we are in Deaf City. Ha, ha."

Madeleine stares at her mother for a while and starts to cry.

"Hey," Eliza gestures amazed. She taps her husband on the arm.

"Look, Madeleine is crying."

"Yes, why?" Louis replies, a bit disturbed. Eliza puts her arm around the shoulders of her eldest and asks what is going on.

"Mum, it's so quiet here. I cannot hear anything at all!"

Madeleine continues to cry. Dominique and Jean are also crying. Grandpa Hinault asks his daughter: "What is happening. Why do they all cry?"

After a while he asks the children, "You do hear the birds?"

"Yes, Grandpa, yes, but…" Madeleine replies.

Then they all walk a little further, until Eliza points with her hand to a street sign. "Avenue of Deafness."

Louis responds, "Ah, we have taken a wrong road. There I see the center."

In the distance, they see a large sign on the roof of a big building. "Ray Holcomb Hotel," it says.

"Yes, we are there," Hinault nods, relieved. His face looks white from fatigue.

Fifteen minutes later, when they are in the entrance hall on the sixth floor of the flat, Madeleine says, "There is house number 657!"

The whole family is finally at the door and Louis takes the pass out of his breast pocket and waves it with some panache. A few seconds later, the doorway gates move upward and the door in the furnished room opens. Suddenly a screen lights up on the beautifully tiled wall. Louis and Eliza are standing right next to it and are a bit startled. They then read on the screen, "Welcome to Surdiopolis. Have fun in our home."

The whole family smiles at each other and exchanges glances, aware of the fact that they are on holiday.

In the evening Mr. and Mrs. Hinault decide not to join in the exploratory walk. They are still too tired from the long journey. Louis and Eliza are happy that the grandparents will look after the children, but Madeleine comes along with them.

After taking the elevator down, they step outside onto the large and wide Abbé Charles Michel de l'Epée Square, the heart of Surdiopolis. The tourists notice how Surdiopolis handles the construction of streets. So, they are very wide and functional. They see sidewalks at busy stores move in one direction, leading to the central parking lot. Very handy. That way, customers do not have to carry their purchases. They can just put it on the moving floor. Eliza suspects that the sidewalk doesn't move when the shops are closed.

Then Eliza, Louis, and Madeleine arrive at a corner of the square. They want to absorb everything, houses, buildings, and the people with their gesticulating hands. People with black, white, red-brown, and yellow skin. They are all there. Surdiopolis is truly a universal city, Eliza thinks in amazement.

"Can we shop?" Madeleine asks a little later. Louis' fingers spell, "Okay."

Eliza laughs for a moment and dreams. "What would the stores look like from the inside? Would they be as much fun as those in France?"

Through the mall, they enter a department store. A moment later, Eliza collides with a man, and she says in French, "Pardon, Monsieur."

Suddenly she realizes that she can keep her mouth shut, because anyone she might bump into is likely also deaf.

"Excuse me," she gestures quickly. The man smiles and says with his hands, while shaking his head, "I beg your pardon, my dear French friends."

Louis is watching the conversation and his eyes open wide in amazement.

"No!" he shakes his head. Eliza notices and quickly looks at the stranger.

"But that's Harold!"

The tall man laughs and gestures, "Yes, it's me!"

Louis embraces him exuberantly since they have not seen each other for a long time. Eliza only gets a courteous kiss from the Englishman.

Harold invites them to come with him. "Let's go to the restaurant for a cup of coffee."

Louis nods enthusiastically and then asks Harold, his friend from London, whether Alice is with him.

"Yes, yes!"

He points to the bent over figure at the porcelain department of the department store. Eliza beckons her daughter to walk with her and taps the unsuspecting woman's shoulder. She slowly turns her head and her eyes look somewhat irritable. She has been busy studying Cheshire porcelain.

Eliza just smiles, knowing that Alice will be very happy to see her again. Her friend's eyes open wide.

"Eliza, how did you get here?!"

Then they embrace. "Are you alone? Are you divorced?" Alice asks quickly.

"No. My Louis is in the restaurant with Harold right now."

It's rewarding to see Alice's face, because at first, she looks just normal, and then, because of Eliza's answer, bright red, out of shame.

They sit all together in the restaurant. Harold talks a lot with his friend, while the women and Madeleine listen.

"Are you on holiday here?" Eliza asks Alice.

Alice looks at her friend, puzzled. "Holiday? No, we have been living here for a year now. Oh, are you here on holiday?"

"Yes, exactly," Louis says, gesturing in the conversation. "Frankly, we are thinking about emigrating here. Now, we can see in advance what the city is like."

"Yes, yes," Harold's clenched fist goes up and down.

"Very sensible, but not necessary. Life here is wonderful here, isn't it?"

He looks at his wife, who then nods fiercely with her finely shaped face. Harold smiles broadly while his glasses reflect the restaurant's artificial light.

Madeleine has spent a long time following the conversation in sign language. But she cannot stand it any longer and taps her mother's arm. "What is Alice saying? I cannot understand her so well."

"Well, we were talking about our holiday, and Harold and Alice have been living here for a year."

"Oh, yes, and Alice asked something about Paris."

"Do you want to know what it was?"

Madeleine shakes her head, staring thoughtfully at a funny bulging lamp that hangs above the circle of the people sitting further on. Suddenly she gestures, "Auntie Alice, I remember that we stayed with you in London five years ago. I know that your daughter is called Priscilla. How is she now?"

Alice nods and congratulates Madeleine for her good memory and says, "Yes, she is here and she is doing well."

152

After a while of a friendly chat, the couples split up, having made a new appointment to visit Harold and Alice's place.

The next day, Eliza and Louis decide to visit the town hall. Their children and Eliza's parents are also coming along. After some searching and some chats with deaf people, they find a space where information about the city can be found.

In one of the halls they find models of the different neighborhoods of the city. While Eliza is looking at one of them, she indeed notices a neighborhood in the shape of a letter, as spelled by hand. On the wall there is also a brightly lit information screen.

Eliza reads that different neighborhoods harbor the inhabitants of their own nationality. For example, there is a German-speaking district in the city, another district is French-speaking and there is also an English-speaking district. Particularly useful, Eliza thinks, because many local shops have products that come from the respective countries. There is a counter in one corner for buying an apartment in the French-speaking district.

"Shall we have a look?" Eliza asks Louis, her face red from all the excitement. Standing at the desk they see many photos of houses on the wall. They also note that the sales person uses his hands to talk to someone next to them.

As soon as the customer is finished, Louis and Eliza turn to the sales person for general information. They learn from him that a new neighborhood is being built. Eliza responds in surprise, "Really?! So, there will be space for more deaf people here?"

The smooth face of the salesman radiates and he says, "Yes. You do not live here?"

Louis laughs and says that they are tourists.

"Yes. What country do you come from? Is it okay to ask?"

"Yes, we are from Paris," says Louis with a proud smile.

Suddenly the presenter claps both hands at the same time. He expresses astonishment and introduces himself as Monsieur Renaud, who was born in Boulogne sur Mer.

"Really?" Louis marvels. "You do not look like a Frenchman."

The salesman smiles professionally and says, "My mother is Swedish by birth."

Eliza and Louis nod and continue to obtain the necessary information about a house. Then Louis feels the light vibration of his wristwatch on his skin.

"Come, it's time. We will go to Harold now."

"That's true: time flies. We can come back here, can't we?" says Eliza with a visible sigh.

After searching for the street where Harold and Alice live, they finally find the address. It's 47, Helen Keller Road in neighborhood C.

Louis, Eliza, and their children arrive at the house. Louis positions himself in such a way that the camera above the door is focused on him and he makes a certain gesture that he had agreed with Harold in advance. Yes, it works. The door opens slowly and the family only sees empty space inside. The Mistinquet family goes in and waits.

Then the inner door swings open. Yes, Harold and Alice are there to welcome their visitors. When they have all found a seat in the living room, Eliza begins with a question about the empty space, where they all had to wait earlier.

Alice nods and her mouth moves in annoyance. "Sorry, that is not fun, but necessary and safe for us as residents of area C."

Louis and Eliza nod and feel overwhelmed. Eliza says she cannot understand why the security system should function like this and asks whether this is meant against burglary.

"Yes, and not only that. There is more. There is a community of infamous criminals about ten kilometers from here."

"Eh, never heard of it," Louis responds dismayed.

"That's right. It was a secret of the United Nations, and recently it leaked, so we got the security system for our neighborhood. That's why we got the 'Safety-system of the United Nations' as a gift for Surdiopolis."

Eliza hisses in astonishment. "That's nice," is her ironic view.

She then takes a cup of tea from the table. It strikes her how wonderful the tea aroma smells. It's pure English.

"Did you not know that Harold is the head of the Security Department of Surdiopolis?" Alice asks with a proud smile.

Louis and Eliza's eyes widen in wonder.

"No. I didn't know that."

"I did know that you wanted to get this job. Is that right?"

Harold laughs and says that is true and he would never have gotten such a job in England.

Alice joins in and says, "That's what I mean. It's great to live and work here. Everyone will see his or her childhood wish come true. Come, shall we go into the garden?"

"Oh, how beautiful," Eliza says.

Harold and Alice laugh with pride, while the sun shines on their faces. The garden itself is not that big or wide. But what the garden displays to the visitors is really beautiful. Lots of red roses, which can only be grown by the English.

Louis starts to ask about the labor situation in Surdiopolis.

"Well…I am a security man and I do not know much about it. By chance I read in the Surdiopolis Post yesterday, that there is a shortage…" Harold deliberately waits a moment. "…a shortage of psychologists and construction workers."

Louis just jumps on the lawn and screams. Madeleine hears it and she walks over to her father and asks what the matter is. Louis laughs and says, "Did I shout so loudly?"

"Well, yes, but why?"

"Just because." Louis teases after a moment of silence.

Madeleine shrugs and joins her brothers again.

Louis looks at his friend and asks, "Really? I mean, does the city really need psychologists?"

Harold pulls an impatient face. "I think I made that clear, right?"

He walks back inside and along the wall, because of his body heat, a screen of forty by forty lights up and the buttons are suddenly visible.

Seeing five screens simultaneously lit elicits many questions from Louis and Eliza. They have never seen anything like this.

"It is certainly very expensive?" Louis asks.

"What do you mean?"

"Well, those five screens…"

Harold and Alice laugh at the same time and shake their heads.

"It costs us nothing! Free! Service from the city administration. Well no, actually, it's a gift from UNESCO."

"Really?" Eliza gestures with her eyes wide open in disbelief.

Harold asks for her opinion. "Do you see this as a sop for us inhabitants of the deaf city?"

Eliza has to laugh and nods.

"You see, Alice, I'm right after all. I do not like it. We have enough money ourselves and happy to spend it. Here, you have little chance to do so, because we get so many donations from the hearing world for Surdiopolis…" Harold says, somewhat strained.

Louis and Eliza are very surprised and can't imagine that it happens that way.

"How do they work, those five screens on the wall? With us in Paris we only have one TV set on the wall."

"How does it work, you mean?" asks Harold. Louis nods. "This system was devised by a deaf man who has lived here from the beginning of the deaf city."

"Oh, how nice. What's his name?" Eliza asks.

"Olivier de Groot. I met him at the recreation center last week."

"How old is he?"

"Well, I do not know. He seems to me to be a sixty-year-old man and he's struggling a little. The electronics industry in South Africa loves him and sponsors all his work."

"Is he a South African by birth?"

"No, he is Dutch."

"Great!" Louis gestures with his thumb.

After a moment of silence, Harold presses a button and types something. Louis reads the text about employment and his own opportunities here, and says, "Yes, you're right. Oh, what a wonderful chance for me to work here!"

Harold believes that the deaf residents of the city sometimes feel homesick for their own country and that they may therefore need spiritual help.

"Ah, yes, that's possible. Strange, I never have thought about that possibility before. So, there's plenty of work to do, I believe…Home sickness happens to be the subject of my final thesis during my studies at Gallaudet University. So here is my life's work, don't you think, Eliza?"

She smiles at him and then abruptly turns to Harold and asks, "Is it true that Surdiopolis needs deaf education at high school level?"

Louis responds in surprise. "Why?"

"Because I would like to teach.

"Yes, yes, you're right. I'm also curious about Harold's answer."

"No, we do not have high school education for the deaf here. Maybe in a few years' time. That's what my friend says. He is chairman here; I mean from the ward C."

Louis and Eliza nod slowly.

Before Eliza gets a chance to say more, she sees her youngest son crying in the garden. She beckons him with her hand. "Come."

Harold immediately understands that the children are getting bored and goes to the wall.

Later the children are enjoying a movie, which is being shown on all five screens at the same time. But the subtitles are different. You can read subtitles in English, French and German. On one screen, however, the official sign language can be seen.

Alice gestures, "It's time for the world news. Do you want to watch it?"

"Yes, I'm curious about it," Eliza exclaims enthusiastically with her hands.

The screen flashes and lights up after some seconds. A very modernly dressed woman appears, gesturing very quickly. Louis shakes his head but says nothing. Alice notices it, and she switches to the French sign language screen. This shows another woman, unmistakably a Frenchwoman.

"Ha," says Louis, putting his thumb up.

After a few stories, news about Paris follows. Louis and Eliza stand up and watch attentively. At some point, the woman on the TV talks about the Eiffel Tower, which has started to rust badly. The city council has decided to dismantle it to the bottom for overhaul, starting next month. But Madeleine, who follows this news in sign language, suddenly bursts into tears. Her hands cover her face.

Then she gestures quickly and carelessly to her parents, "Oh, awful! The Eiffel Tower is being demolished! Forever!" She walks out of the room into the garden, followed by the eyes of her uncomprehending parents.

Louis then looks at his wife with raised eyebrows, "What's with Madeleine?"

Eliza walks to the garden. She is curious about the reason for her daughter's outburst. A moment later Eliza comes back with a broad smile.

"Yes...that's a nice joke." She deliberately waits before continuing. "Madeleine misunderstood the news about the Eiffel Tower, and thought they were planning to destroy this beautiful tower. Ha, ha."

After a while, Louis says that they need to be going.

"Already? Stay here for a while, or do you have an appointment?"

"No," says Louis.

Eliza says, "I have so many questions about life here, but we do not want to tire you out with this."

"No, not at all. You are our best friends. We can help you. Okay?"

Louis and Eliza nod and Eliza asks, "For example, I want to know about the administration of Surdiopolis. Can you tell us about it, Harold?"

The man from the security service sits upright and gestures.

"Surdiopolis has a council of seven, headed by the mayor, with a president in each district. For the city, he or she represents on behalf of the people of his district. Did I say that right, Alice?"

Her hand indicates, "Okay."

Eliza indicates that this form of governance is simple but effective and that it is not new. She then asks, "Who is the mayor? Where does he come from?"

"Boris Perznikov from Ukraine. He is a very gifted and warm human."

Eliza nods slowly while her thinking wrinkles are visible to Louis. She then waves her hand at Harold.

"Fine. I'm glad I know that now. Would it be possible to arrange an appointment to meet with Mr. Perznikov?"

"Yes, that is very well possible, because tomorrow morning I have an appointment with the municipal executive about the security of the city. I will of course mention you. May I ask what you want to talk to Mr. Perznikov about?"

"Yes, I want to know if there is work for me in Surdiopolis and I would really like to talk to the mayor myself."

"I'll do it tomorrow."

Harold asks, "Eliza, you have studied what…? I'll have to tell the mayor who you are and what you do, etc."

Eliza sighs with satisfaction and passes on her credentials. "Firstly, I became deaf when I was three years old and it is exactly ten years ago this year that I got my degree in sociology and political science as a secondary subject at the Sorbonne. Now I work on an urban project. Our government is investigating the movement of social groups within human society."

Alice is very impressed and gestures and nods, asking, "How is that possible? You are completely deaf. Can you just deal with hearing people, if you are doing fieldwork?"

Eliza smiles but her eyes contradict. "How do they work, those five screens on the wall? With us in Paris we only have one TV set on the wall."

"Yes, I always wanted to do that, but yes, I only do the office work. The communication often causes problems."

Harold says that the French often speak too quickly and in haste.

"Really?" says Louis. Irony shows on his face.

The next day, Eliza gets a new hairdo in a beauty salon. She hopes to make a good impression on the mayor with whom she has a business appointment. When Louis and his wife meet each other at an agreed time on the street, named after a pioneer in the field of sign language research, he gestures, "How beautiful you are. I hardly recognize you."

Louis looks for a long time at the new but familiar face of his wife.

"It's very good," Louis adds.

Eliza smiles somewhat shyly.

Over the course of the afternoon, Louis and Eliza pick up their children. They are busy jumping on the trampoline at the sports center. The children are having a lot of fun. Especially Dominique, who is angry when his parents say that they have to go home.

"Come on, we're going to see Grandpa and Grandma," Louis tells them with a friendly face. "Now we have to go to the town hall."

Madeleine looks surprised at her father and asks what they are going to do there. Eliza sighs and says that there is little time to explain.

But her daughter suddenly taps on her mother's arm. "Oh, how beautiful you are! How is that possible? You did not do it yourself?"

"No. That's right; I've been to a hairdresser."

Madeleine nods and asks if she should go to that hairdresser herself.

Louis grabs her by the shoulder and says, "You're okay. You're too young. You look gorgeous enough!"

While chatting they arrive at the Ray Holcomb Hotel and they drop the children off.

Exactly at half past six the door of Boris Perznikov's office swings open and on the TV screen he has already seen that his visitors have arrived. He stands up and walks around his desk. Eliza sees the corpulent man arriving and immediately feels that Harold has not said too much about the personality of her host.

The Ukrainian gestures quietly, and now and then he stops to give his guests the opportunity to understand him. But Louis does not have any trouble in that respect. It can clearly be seen that ASL is used here.

"Just sit down. Would you like coffee or tea?"

Perznikov taps on a small device and after a while a woman comes with a large tray with coffee, tea, sugar, and milk. The mayor starts to tell about the initially difficult construction of the city. He does so in a few sketches, which Louis and Eliza find easy to understand.

"Is it clear for you?" asks Perznikov.

"Yes, I have no more questions," says Eliza.

The mayor nods and leans backward.

"What is the reason for your visit?" he asks suddenly.

Eliza's demeanor betrays some nervousness. It is no small matter that she has an audience with this man.

After a long consultation with her husband, she has decided she wants to go to work immediately after their vacation time, here in the city. In fact, Louis also wants that.

Eliza tells the mayor that she wants to work in Surdiopolis.

"So, do you have the papers?"

Eliza hears the long-awaited question with a smile. She had been clever enough to bring her papers in case they would be necessary.

"Yes, here they are."

162

"Thank you, Madame." He studies Eliza's French credentials. It takes a while but at last the city's boss has finished.

"My French is not as good as it used to be," he apologizes with a mere gesture and a smile. "But, you have a great background for the position of deputy mayor!"

Eliza suddenly blushes. She is really pleased. For her it is the first time that an official has given her a sincere compliment.

"Madame Mistinquet," Perznikov spells this name quickly and flawlessly with his fingers, "you first have to gain some experience at the district councils of the city.
What would you think about first getting an internship? I have a proposal. You'll work as an intern for the two council's internships for a month and then work here for a week."

Eliza just nods. She is perfectly happy with the proposal. However, the mayor holds his finger up and gestures that it has to remain a total secret.

Louis is surprised about the speed of the decision by the mayor and dares to ask, "Excuse me. Do you not need to consult with the responsible people of the Councils first?"

Eliza looks at her husband, disturbed.

"Aha! I understand. Democracy… Yes, it was invented by the French. That is your right, but it has been a while since the internship was made available. Nobody wants or has been able to do it until now," says Perznikov.

Eliza and Louis nod.

"What do you think of my proposal, Madame Mistinquet?"

Eliza says that for her it is great, but she needs some time to finish her job in Paris. She gestures to her husband, "What do you think?"

"Well! You now have a job as deputy mayor. What do I think? I'm sure you will have a fine job here," gestures Louis with a radiant face.

"Yes, you're right."

Eliza turns to the mayor and says, "Oh, I'm only realizing now, Mister Perznikov. Thank you so much for the job offer. I'm not sure yet when we can move here. My husband is also looking for a job."

Perznikov stares at Louis and says, "Maybe that can wait for a while. What your wife will do for the city has the highest priority. The city is expanding and I really need more assistance."

After a moment of thinking, the mayor asks, "What work do you do in Paris?"

"I'm a pastoral worker and a psychologist, specializing in people with homesickness," says Louis. "I think there must be a lot of deaf people here with homesickness. Is that right?"

Perznikov nods violently and believes there is also a hidden sadness among the people here, and they much need such a psychologist.

"I cannot promise anything, but I'll speak with the people in the health care department."

"That's fine," Louis says with a visible sigh. "I am very grateful to you and I'll wait for your answer. But there is one more thing, if you have a few more minutes to listen to me?"

Eliza looks at her husband, puzzled but says nothing.

"What is it?" asks the mayor.

"Our children need to continue learning in regular education. I wonder whether this city has such a school."

Eliza's face beams again when she looks at Louis and says that it is very important indeed. She awaits the answer with suspense.

Perznikov strokes his fat cheek with his hand and gestures, "How long have you been in our town?"

"How long? Oh, you mean how long have we been here as tourists?"

"Yes," the hand of the mayor moves.

"Several days now."

"Monsieur Mistinquet, I assume that you and your wife have not seen the city school yet."

"That's right," Louis replies with his hand. He moves his thumb and index finger several times, a typically French gesture.

Perznikov says, "The city school is functioning properly. And so far, we have a total of forty-six pupils, taught by two women from Ireland. They are both daughters of a deaf couple called O'Reill."

"That is good to know." Eliza continues, "When these children finish school, what will happen to them? Is there high school education for them here?"

"Well, we don't know yet. This needs to be looked into. We have only recently started here."

Louis then asks Perznikov whether there will be a school for deaf pupils.

"A good question. But we don't have one yet!"

"No?!" Eliza asks, dismayed.

"Why could this be, you think?" the mayor asks with a twinkle in his eyes. He is challenging Eliza.

After briefly pondering, Eliza suggests that maybe the World Federation of the Deaf is opposed to starting a deaf school in Surdiopolis.

"Well, no Perznikov laughs and says that the city has no money for a school.

"But there are deaf children enrolled at the city school. They are taught by a deaf teacher. Their number is now twelve. If there are more than thirty in Surdiopolis, we'll go to UNESCO for financial assistance."

Eliza and Louis nod slowly. They understand that Surdiopolis is still developing in all areas and that more time is needed to start something new.

"Okay," the mayor suddenly gestures. "I'll go and make an appointment with the city school for you."

Without waiting for a response from Eliza and Louis, he taps on a keyboard. Then he gestures toward a monitor that is laid in front of him on the desk. Eliza and Louis look at each other and wait.

"Okay! Tomorrow you can meet with two women from the city school. I myself have four children and I know it is important for them to get a good education."

"Yes, that's great," his guests nod.

"Will I see you, Madame Mistinquet, tomorrow morning at 10 a.m.? We have a gathering with the District Councils. I assume you want to come to it. It is public."

Eliza's face radiates and she asks where the meeting will be held. The mayor is smiling and it's obvious that he feels content.

"In the Abraham Lincoln room." He points with his finger over his visitors and gestures at the same time. "Second door on the right." Then he stands up, indicating that the conversation has ended.

In the elevator of the state-of-the-art building in which the City Government is seated, Louis chats with his wife.

During a break in their chatter, Eliza's hand rests on her husband's arm. "Mayor Perznikov has mentioned the Drug Rehabilitation Center. Do you not think that is strange? What deaf people would make use of this Center?"

Louis nods with emphasis and says that perhaps it would also be his task to help such people with their homesickness.

Three months later, the Mistinquet family is preparing for the permanent emigration to Surdiopolis, to their new house on the

Avenue Pierre Desloges in the French district. One evening, Louis and Eliza clean up many things that are no longer needed. Old documents go in a shredder. The rest they put in moving boxes.

A small blue booklet suddenly attracts Eliza's attention. In the booklet, she finds an article, held together with a rusty clip. It is circled with a red pen. But this article is in a foreign language. The content makes her curious enough that she takes the booklet to her husband's work room.

"Look, I have an article here. Can you read what it says?"

"Well, anyone can read…"

"No, look at it. It is written in a foreign language!"

Louis is now attentive and tries to read it to figure out its origin. His shoulders are going up. He, too, does not know.

"Who sent it to you at the time?"

Eliza's eyebrows go up while she's thinking. Suddenly, her face brightens. "I remember! This little book was given to me by my dad's friend in Brussels. I believe his name was Dupont. Yes, that's exactly right. Look."

Louis looks at the last page and spots the name.

It must be Dutch. Look at those yellowed red marks. That makes me curious," says Eliza, gesturing.

Louis laughs and advises her to put this article in a translation machine. "Then you'll know what you're reading."

Eliza, however, looks at the big French-made wall clock, and wrinkles up her nose, "It's a bit, isn't it?"

Louis says, "Just give it to me. It is very easy."

"Really? Then I'll do it myself."

"Okay," Louis' hand says.

A few seconds later, it comes back like a slice of bread from a toaster. Louis takes a sheet of paper out of the printer and wants to read the content, but Eliza snatches it out of his hand and says with a laugh, "Me first, okay?"

Eliza first reads the title, which is very important: "ORALISM...THE RIGHT METHOD?" by Surdianus.

She says, "Oralism...? That is a method in the deaf education to learn to speak and to understand spoken words and lips. So, there is no sign language in the school. That is the policy."

Louis and Eliza find it hard to read; many important words have not been translated because of the age of the paper, but they try reading anyhow. It takes a lot of effort.

"In addition, deaf adults notice from the behavior of former pupils of the school taught with the oral method, that from an early age, they have used their typical cultural sign language very little."

Many words are lost for the two readers. Eliza and her husband read further. They are slightly annoyed. They arrive at the last sentences of the article, which states, "Bilingualism in international deaf education: international sign language and the regular language of a country are the perfect means of communication for deaf pupils. The same applies also with respect the spoken language in regular education. After the deafness of their infant has been established, hearing parents should be given the opportunity right away to follow a communication course in sign language. This will allow deaf infants to be offered the language from their parents. Furthermore, deaf people with a teaching degree are capable of teaching in the bilingual deaf education."

The author of the article further writes, "Finally, an important fact needs to be mentioned. Deaf education and hearing parents should be more active in obtaining information from the Deaf world, which, after all, has a full culture, identity, and history.

"The oral method is irrefutably not appropriate for the upbringing of children and in the education of a deaf child and can therefore be considered a form of EDUCATIONAL CRIME."

"So, it is!" says Louis to Eliza, who is lazily reclining on the bed.

He believes that the anonymous writer is right. The content of this article should have been published in the last century in all countries where oralism reigns supreme.

"Yes, it is too bad that it has not happened but we, deaf people, have known this for a long time. What we experienced and what we thought, in fact, contributed to the idea of building a city such as Surdiopolis," says Eliza.

"Exactly. But I do now feel relieved."

"How so?" Eliza says.

"Well, until now I had the feeling that maybe emigrating to this city is like a flight from reality for many deaf people," gestures Louis. "I mean, because of the many problems deaf people encounter in their countries."

"As far as a flight is concerned, I don't feel it that way. I have been offered a magnificent job in Surdiopolis," says Eliza.

It seems that Eliza is almost asleep because her eyes are closed, Louis notices. He continues to say, "Very many deaf people have had a lot to endure from the hearing people, who do not understand what it is like to be deaf."

Eliza nods and says, "Well, it will be a heaven on earth for the both of us when we move to Surdiopolis tomorrow. Why wouldn't we be allowed to be there?!"

Her husband nods enthusiastically and lies down again. Within half an hour the future inhabitants of the deaf city are relaxing in the warm darkness of the bedroom.

17.   Visible Alarm

Alarm!

One morning, a red light suddenly flashes on and off. In the workspace of "Insula", the office building, built on large pillars of what once the deaf association, the deaf-born system administrator is frightened by the fearsome flashes. It is the first time this has happened! Therefore, Henry hesitates a fraction of a second. Could it be accidental? The fear suddenly resonates in full force within him. Hastily he gestures to a few of his colleagues who are in the same room with him.

"Full alert! Look, the light is on! We must leave!"

Henry does not wait and leaves the building, very quickly for his age, via the stairs. He notices immediately that the rain is dripping down his face. Too bad I did not

bring my coat with me, goes through his head.

Only when he is hundreds of meters away from the building at L'Abbé Charles Michel de l'Epée Square, he realizes that he is one of the people in front. Curiously, he turns around and sees that not all, but only a dozen colleagues come running after him. He is very tired. Suddenly he feels with his feet that the ground begins to shake violently, and he feels something touch his hair. It must be the air pressure, Henry thinks in shock.

Near the Thomas Davidson Gallery, where the works of world-famous deaf artists from the middle of the 21st century are permanently exhibited, Henry looks for cover under a very large tree. But some branches come falling down as if they are chestnuts in a storm.

Henry is a system administrator and when he sees what is left of the beautiful building, it goes through his head that this could be another terrorist act, this time probably by the Legios group of previously hearing young people.

Henry feels anger rise. A few days ago, this group announced in the newspaper that if the provincial government would not deal with their demands, the group would carry out a violent act. Henry has forgotten what the demands were.

Since 2067, the office building, "Insula" has been heavily guarded. But now, on 21 September, 2070, the terrorist group has apparently found a weak link and the building has exploded!

Standing behind a shelter, Henry sees some colleagues who belong to the voluntary fire guard desperately walking back and forth. Because radioactive radiation is released, they are forced to stay at a safe distance from the exploded building and therefore are unable to do anything. Henry can sympathize with their powerlessness. The building quickly turns into a ruin, full of swirling smoke. The look of it shocks him deeply. It looks like Hiroshima in the last century. He wonders how many deaths there will be.

It does not rain anymore and there is almost no wind. Next to Henry stands a woman of about twenty-five years old. She is sweating and her cheeks are wet with tears. He knows her; she is newly married and works in the canteen on the ninth floor. He does not dare to ask why she is crying.

Moments later she tells him in jerky gestures that her husband might be lying under the rubble. Henry frowns and tries to remember what her husband looks like.

"John, my husband with the big mustache, you remember him?"

Henry thinks long and nods; he remembers the man. The woman, slightly shorter than he, continues with stiff gesticulating, "I told John to leave straight away, but he said…"

Her sobbing prevents her from saying any more. Henry waits patiently and then she says, "John said, 'Yes, my darling, I'm coming home, but I need to finish off something here...'"

Henry suspects that John is now indeed no longer alive. There is no way he could be, he thinks in silence. He puts his arms around the woman to comfort her. Suddenly he sees Maureen and Eric, his adult children, and Heather, his wife, arrive. The woman from the canteen walks away slowly. Henry then feels his wife's arms around him. That feels nice. Eric asks his father how what happened to the office building is even possible. He talks with moving mouth and hands.

Just like his sister, he has been using sign language since his early years. Maureen and Eric use every resource in order to communicate. This is called Total Communication.

For a few years—to be exact, since April of the year 2065, after the great disaster—all the people on Earth are forced to use the method of sign language. A sound attack suddenly happened everywhere on Earth. This was a great disaster for any hearing person. Henry and his family can still very clearly remember the attack. One night the earth had started to tremble with a hell of a noise, which lasted four days and nights. He had felt the strange sound along the ground and via vibrations through objects. He noted how this sound tortured both hearing and hard of hearing people. Also, their animals were affected. Headphones for protection against the loud sound did not help.

It seemed as if there was an invisible inferno. So, all hearing people were exposed to an exceptionally loud sound. They still don't know where the sound came from. Only the people who at that time were already deaf had no problems. Unfortunately, Heather also lost her hearing. But Tara, Maureen's youngest daughter, who was born in February 2066, is able to hear. So, the world will have people with good hearing again in the long run.

A few days after this sound disaster, Heather realized that her highly advanced hearing aid was now redundant. Like many people, she was naturally full of anger and deep disappointment. Listening to music and speaking on her phone were things of the past.

One afternoon Heather flung her hearing aid on the tiles in the garden. Henry was shocked but wisely kept his mouth shut, even though deep in his heart he found it a big waste since it had cost so much money! He remembers vividly how Heather had snapped at him in those days:

"So, you now have what you wanted all along! Everyone is now deaf!"

Henry had put his hands up in surprised indignation. But, it was true; long ago in despair he had said that he wished everyone would go deaf. He had completely forgotten…

Since the days of the noise disaster, total deafness has forced everyone to learn how to use the sign language.

As a result, the method of Total Communication flourishes as never before, but the element of speech is greatly neglected. Institutions where courses in sign language could be learned have sprung up everywhere.

The exploded office building was also such an institution. Learning sign language is a slow process, because a lot of practice is required, and people have to adapt to their new situation of being deaf.

"Shortly after the sound disaster, our office was specially adapted for all employees," said Henry to his son. "But most colleagues forgot that everything they do is because of what they see rather than hear. Therefore, there were only few people who left the building in time."

A moment later, Eric says that the Legios group has struck again.

"How do you know?" his father asks with hand gestures.

"I saw it on the TV screen of the Mytrose," Eric replies. "So many people had gathered there that I wondered what was happening."

Henry nods but says nothing. His brain is working at full speed and moments later he says, "There has to have been a man with a miniature bomb, perhaps hidden in the heel of his shoe."

"How do you know that?" Maureen asks immediately.

Henry tells with quiet gestures that this assertion was made by a scholar on the internet. "It is possible to make a time bomb that can get around any surveillance for radioactive substances and similar things. Thus, the chance of discovery in such a large building…"

The hands of Heather and the children agree several times. While the sun breaks through the clouds, they stand silently, staring at the ruin.